Tricia's Got
T-R-O-U-B-L-E!

The
Twelve Candles Club

Also by Elaine L. Schulte

Joanna

Tricia's Got
T-R-O-U-B-L-E!

Elaine L. Schulte

BETHANY HOUSE PUBLISHERS
MINNEAPOLIS, MINNESOTA 55438

Tricia's Got Trouble!
Copyright © 1993
Elaine Schulte

Cover illustration by Andrea Jorgenson

Published by Bethany House Publishers
A Ministry of Bethany Fellowship International
11400 Hampshire Avenue South
Minneapolis, Minnesota 55438
www.bethanyhouse.com

Printed in the United States of America by
Bethany Press International, Minneapolis, Minnesota 55438

Library of Congress Cataloging-in-Publication Data
Schulte, Elaine L.
    Tricia's got trouble / Elaine Schulte.
        p. cm. — (The Twelve Candles Club ; bk. 4)
    Summary: Tricia, a member of the Twelve Candles Club, investigates the theft of two valuable paintings and tries to persuade her father to come back home.
    [1. Mystery and detective stories. 2. Fathers and daughters—Fiction. 3. Clubs—Fiction. 4. Christian life—Fiction.] I. Title.
II. Title: Tricia's got trouble. III. Series: Schulte, Elaine L. Twelve Candles Club ; 4.
PZ7.S3867Tr   1993
[Fic]—dc20   93–5339
                                                              CIP
ISBN 1–55661–253–2   AC

To NCPC's Prime Timers

San Diego's CYT

and Lamb's Players

and to the real Martha Jane (Hayden)

ELAINE L. SCHULTE is the well-known author of twenty-five novels for women and children. Over a million copies of her popular books have been sold. She received a Distinguished Alumna Award from Purdue University as well as numerous other awards for her work as an author. After living in various places, including several years in Europe, she and her husband make their home in San Diego, California, where she writes full time.

CHAPTER

1

Places. . . ! Camera. . . ! Action. . . !"

Tricia Bennett pounded a *knock-knock, knock-knock-knock-knock* on the front door of her best friend's house. "Time for the Twelve Candles Club to go into party-helper mode! There are going to be two hundred guests!"

"Whoa! Two hundred guests!" Becky yelled through the screen of her first-floor bedroom window. "Be out in a minute!"

"Mom and I will be waiting in our van," Tricia answered.

She headed for her own driveway, only a few feet across the lawn. Two hundred guests in the midst of valuable paintings didn't seem like much compared to her own family troubles. But this Fourth of July job at the fabulous LeRoy estate was another great break for the Twelve Candles Club—and she'd dwell on that. Besides, working at a party with a jazz band and fireworks was sure to be fun.

The garage door to the Bennetts' two-story, peach-colored house grrrrumphed open, and Mom backed out their maroon minivan. As usual, her mom was glad to drive her along with Becky, Jess, and Cara to their job, since they were twelve years old and none of them drove yet.

Ever since school had let out for the summer, there'd been plenty of interesting jobs for them: baby-sitting, Morning Fun for Kids, party-helping, car-washing, and even housecleaning. The Twelve Candles Club had zoomed off like a rocket—mainly because of Becky's wacko dog-chase being shown on the TV news.

Tricia slid open the side door of the minivan and climbed into the middle seat. "Becky's on her way."

Mom lifted her wavy brown hair off her neck. It was hot for July, even in California. "No hurry."

Her eyes met Tricia's in the rearview mirror, and Tricia was glad to see that her mother's blue eyes weren't teary. Sometimes they were, ever since Dad had left them and moved to Los Angeles two months ago. But Mom looked wistful as she remarked, "Wish *I* were going to a party with fireworks and all."

"At least Suzanne and Bryan will see fireworks at the fair," Tricia said of her seven-year-old sister and five-year-old brother. "It was nice of Becky's mom to take them along with Amanda and Mr. Bradshaw. Maybe you should have asked to go."

Mom gave a laugh. "I'd say Mrs. Hamilton and Mr. Bradshaw already have enough company—three kids with them on a date!"

Tricia smiled herself. "I guess so."

After a moment, Tricia leaned over the front seat and checked herself in the rearview mirror: reddish blond hair streaming neatly across her shoulders, green eyes sparkling, tiny freckles sprinkled over the bridge of her nose. She looked fine, too, like nothing in the world was wrong.

Sitting back, she glimpsed movement at the Hamiltons' front door. "Here comes Becky now."

Becky ran across the lawn from her small Spanish-style house, her long legs pumping under a white skirt and her brown wavy hair bobbing against the shoulders of her white blouse. She hurried around the front of the van, then climbed in next to Tricia. "Sorry to hold you up, Mrs. Bennett. I didn't know we were leaving early."

"No problem," Mom said. "We just felt eager to get going."

Eager wasn't the word for it, Tricia thought, giving Becky the window seat. Since Dad had left them, her family had been downright *jittery*.

"I'd hate to keep you waiting," Becky said.

"I wish everyone were as thoughtful as you, Becky," Mom replied, backing the minivan down the driveway. They turned south down their street, La Crescenta, to pick up Jess McColl and Cara Hernandez, who lived across from each other.

"Here they come!" Tricia exclaimed as Jess and Cara ran from their houses. "Whoa, don't we all look nice in our white blouses and skirts!"

"And our candle medallions around our necks," Becky remarked. "They add a nice artistic touch."

"Which only *you'd* notice," Tricia told her. Becky was the artistic one in the club. She'd already earned lots of money designing and selling her own party invitations. "Well, maybe the LeRoys will notice, since they're art collectors."

"I can't wait to see their fantastic paintings," Becky replied. "They are supposed to be terrific."

Mom slowed the minivan to a stop, and Jess, a short and energetic gymnast, slid open the door and jumped in first, singing out, "Party . . . party . . . fireworks party!" Her hazel eyes sparkling and short brown hair bouncing, she wobbled her head and laughed crazily, making them all laugh with her as she headed for the backseat.

Cara was right behind, her almost-black curly hair pulled back with a white barrette. Still smiling, she rolled her brown eyes at Jess. "Thanks for picking us up, Mrs. Bennett," Cara said, not so shy anymore.

"My pleasure," Mrs. Bennett answered. "I like being part of the excitement."

From the backseat, Jess put in, "My mom says being in the Twelve Candles Club has given us more exciting lives than anyone else in the whole neighborhood."

"So far it has!" Mom laughed. She waited until they were buckled in, then drove off. "Should be interesting, a jazz benefit for the university music department."

"A benefit? You mean everyone has to pay to come?" Jess asked over the rumble of the van.

"Yep," Tricia told her, "in order to raise money for a worthy cause. You know, like the Llewellyns' big western party to raise money for abused kids."

"Guess I still wasn't sure," Jess admitted. "While I'm asking, what's jazz?"

No one answered, so Mom said, "Jazz is part blues, Dixieland, and ragtime music, with a little swing thrown in. It's very popular in places like New Orleans."

"*Veddy* interesting," Jess said comically. "*Veddy* interesting. How'd we ever get this job at the LeRoy estate anyhow?"

Tricia began to bounce with excitement. "Easy. Their caterers didn't know they were supposed to supply serving help, and the LeRoys phoned all around to find some. My Gramp Bennett told them about us. He likes jazz himself, which is how he knows Mr. LeRoy."

"Ministers must have all kinds of interesting friends," Becky remarked.

"You know it," Tricia answered. "Even retired ministers like Gramp. He and Gram are going to be at the party, too. It's supposed to be Brazilian jazz. Can you believe it? The Amazon Jazz Band on the Fourth of July!"

"Sounds different, all right," Cara put in.

Mom turned up Ocean Avenue, leaving Santa Rosita Estates behind them, and Tricia recited in her most dramatic poetry-reading voice, "The jungle is a dark, dank place . . . of thumping drums and slithering snakes . . . of nighttime screams and daytime shakes—"

"*Come on*, Tricia!" Becky exclaimed. "What's that got to do with the LeRoys' jazz party?"

"B-r-a-z-i-l-i-a-n j-u-n-g-l-e-s," Tricia explained, turning her sly jungle-cat smile on them.

"You're making it up," Becky decided.

Tricia nodded. "What'd you expect? I don't know any Brazilian poems—"

"Oh, Tricia, you're *so* dramatic," Jess teased from the backseat.

"Actress . . . actress . . . actress!" Becky and Cara joined in mockingly.

"You're right about that," Tricia agreed. "Besides, I like acting because I can be even more wacko than you guys!"

"More wacko?" Becky asked, staring suspiciously at her friend.

"Wacko! Wacko! Wacko!" Cara and Jess chorused.

Tricia shot Becky a grin. What they didn't know was that her being wacko—and her talent for acting—had helped her forget lately about Dad taking off on their family. In fact, next week she was trying out for the character of Alice in *Alice in Wonderland*.

"Is that weird Odette LeRoy going to be at the party?" Becky asked.

"Let's hope not!" Tricia exclaimed.

She knew why Becky was interested, though. Dad lived in the same Los Angeles condo complex as the LeRoys' way-out, twenty-five-year-old granddaughter, Odette. When Tricia had visited him there a few weeks ago, the oh-so-snooty Odette LeRoy had been just a little too friendly with Dad as they'd lounged around the condo swimming pool, then later when they'd gone out to dinner and to lunch the next day.

As it was, Tricia felt uneasy enough about working for Odette's grandparents. She certainly hoped that Odette LeRoy would not be at the party today. What's more, she hoped that she'd *never* see her again.

Tricia saw Mom glance at her in the rearview mirror, and she was suddenly glad that she hadn't told her mother about Odette LeRoy.

The minivan roared up a winding hillside, where houses stood on acres and acres of land in the midst of orange groves. They weren't development homes like those in Santa Rosita Estates. These houses all looked different from one another, and some could even be called mansions.

After winding through the hills for a long time, Mom

slowed the minivan. "Here we are, ladies. The famous and fabulous LeRoy estate."

"Whoa—look at that!" Jess exclaimed, impressed. And it took a lot to impress her, since she lived in the biggest and nicest house in Santa Rosita Estates.

Tricia craned her neck to look up to the top of a small hill, where she spied a huge white Spanish-style home sprawling across the hilltop among the orange groves. She gazed back down the road at the massive iron gate in front of them. "And— get this—a giant driveway door that swings open like a castle moat gate!"

"Luckily with no water under it," Becky laughed. "Check out the size of that house! We'll wear our feet off to the ankles working there."

"Looks like a setting for a mystery show," Tricia decided. "I've got a feeling this is going to be . . . an interesting job."

"Me too," Becky answered.

Just so it's not too interesting, Tricia thought.

The entry gate had already been swung open to one side of the driveway, and the minivan roared past it. They drove over a black security cord, the kind that rings a warning bell in the house, then they curved around through the orange groves until they arrived at the top of the hill.

A small sign with an arrow spelled out DELIVERIES, and Mom said, "Guess I'd better 'deliver' you back there."

As they drove around to the rear of the house, Tricia couldn't help reciting again, "The jungle is a dark, dank place . . . of thumping drums and slithering snakes . . . nighttime screams and daytime shakes—"

"Stop it, Tricia!" Becky protested. "You're turning a perfectly beautiful house into a spooky place!"

"Sorry," she answered, wishing she didn't feel so peculiar about the LeRoy estate. "It's only my wild imagination."

Mom stopped the minivan at the back door near two other vans. "Looks as if the band and the caterers are already here."

Signs on the vans said, *Amazon Jazz Band* and *Santa Rosita Catering*, and Tricia let out a sigh of relief. "At least it's not Mrs. Wurtzel's catering company."

Jess tugged their minivan's door open. "You're right about that! Mrs. Wurtzel won't be here to grouch at us like at the Llewellyns' or the Tuckers' parties."

They piled out of the minivan and headed for the screened back door. "Hello?" Tricia called into the house. "The Twelve Candles Club reporting for work!"

"Come in!" a pleasant voice answered from inside. "Please let yourselves right in."

They stepped into an enormous, high-ceilinged white kitchen. On the other side of the cooking island a lively lady in a floaty blue summer dress was supervising as three men unloaded boxes of huge bowls and platters. She glanced at the girls, then hurried over to them, smiling. "I'm Mrs. LeRoy, and I'm so grateful you could be here."

"We're ready to work," Tricia announced.

Mrs. LeRoy was gray-haired and petite, but she bustled with energy. "Good," she said. "Mr. LeRoy and I really appreciate your helping us out at the last moment, although I'm afraid you'll be as busy as can be. This is Marta, my housekeeper, who will keep things running smoothly."

"*Buenas tardes*," Marta said. She was about Tricia's mom's age and had beautiful brown eyes and dark curly hair. "We are glad you can help."

"*Buenas tardes*," Tricia replied with her friends, since they all knew that was "good afternoon" in Spanish.

"The caterers will handle the kitchen and put out the buffet foods. As usual, Marta will have to be everywhere. With two hundred guests, both she and I will be giving you directions."

"Two hundred guests!" Jess's eyebrows shot up. "Nobody told me."

"Is that too much for you?" Mrs. LeRoy asked.

Tricia swallowed hard. "We'll be fine," she said, giving Jess a silencing look. "Just fine."

Luckily, Cara kept her mouth shut.

"You must be Reverend Bennett's granddaughter," Mrs. LeRoy said. "You look a bit like him."

"Yes, I'm Tricia Bennett . . . and this is Jess McColl, Cara Hernandez, and Becky Hamilton."

"Don't you girls look nice!" Mrs. LeRoy remarked.

Tricia was thankful that Mrs. LeRoy didn't in any way resemble her granddaughter, the odious Odette. And this part of the house, at least, was light and airy, not a dark, dank place.

"Well, I'd better give you instructions before the guests arrive," Mrs. LeRoy said, getting down to business. "To begin, we'll need two of you sitting near the entry to check off names and hand out name tags until everyone's here. And I need two for helping the caterers to serve and clean up as we go. It's an outdoor party around the pool. . . ."

Her high heels clicked on the white marble floor as they all followed her through a long white hallway with paintings hanging on the walls. Passing by a wide doorway that led out to the pool, Tricia saw the band members setting up their equipment and lots of round tables covered with colorful tablecloths.

"That's Mr. LeRoy talking to the jazz players now." Mrs.

LeRoy nodded toward a short man with gray hair, who waved and turned a welcoming smile on them.

Finally they circled back to the two-story entryway with huge double doors, a white marble floor, and a high dome-shaped skylight in the ceiling. White . . . white . . . everything was white. Tricia darted a glance at her friends, who looked just as impressed as she felt.

Wow! Becky mouthed at her.

Before long, she and Becky were seated behind an antique table that held stick-on tags and lists of names.

"We have two guest lists," Mrs. LeRoy explained, "one with names from A through K, and the other, L to Z. Don't let anyone in who isn't on the list. The lists should give us control over who comes. Be sure to check off names."

"We'll watch like hawks," Tricia promised.

"There's a call button behind you if you need help," Mrs. LeRoy said, pointing out the hidden wall button.

"Who'd come if we pushed it?" Becky asked uneasily.

"Our area's private security patrol," Mrs. LeRoy replied. "And another thing—we've been having a terrible problem with mice getting into the house, not that you can do anything about that. We have, however, acquired two cats."

She glanced out the double doors and her eyes lit on a mostly black cat near the white marble steps. "Well, there's Blackie right now. I'm nervous about keeping the front doors open for guests—and mice—but it wouldn't look very inviting for guests if the doors were shut."

"I guess not," Tricia put in, then saw a calico cat watching them from across the driveway. "There's the other cat."

"Calico," Mrs. LeRoy said and smiled. "We didn't give them very original names."

They all smiled a little, and Mrs. LeRoy must have guessed they felt nervous because she smiled cheerily at them. "You look wonderful in your white outfits and candle medallions. It's a nice touch for the party. Now, Jess and Cara, if you'll come out on the patio with me, I'll show you what to do there."

Moments later, Jess and Cara disappeared around the corner with Mrs. LeRoy, heading in the direction of the kitchen.

Tricia glanced around the enormous white marble entryway and whispered, "Just look at the paintings! It's great art—and *not* copies, either. I can't believe this!"

"I've been looking," Becky answered. "We'd better make very sure no *un*invited guests get in. With hidden call buttons and security guards and all, Mrs. LeRoy must be really worried about burglars." Becky looked awfully serious for a moment. "Besides, that's all we'd need to ruin the club!"

"You're right about that," Tricia answered anxiously. "And we'd better start watching . . . here come the first guests."

CHAPTER

2

*B*efore long, a crowd of guests streamed through the LeRoys' vaulted entryway, and Tricia and Becky were busy greeting them, checking names off the guest list, and handing out the stick-on name tags. Music from the patio filled the air, adding to the excitement.

"Wish we could speed the guests up somehow," Tricia whispered.

"You know it," Becky agreed. "We could use some of those mice scurrying in the doors about now to get everyone moving!"

Tricia gave a laugh. "Wouldn't that be wild?"

After a while, they heard a man's voice in the crowd say, "Well, if those girls aren't a lovely sight."

"Gramp!" Tricia exclaimed.

She craned her neck and spotted him halfway in from the double doors. He looked tall and distinguished with his silvery hair. In his casual shirt and white sport coat, probably no one would even guess he was a retired minister—except maybe by his joyous smile. She beamed at him, then saw Gram Martha-Jane and gave her a little wave.

Finally they made their way up through the crowd to the table and greeted Becky, too. "Hugs later," Tricia told them. "Not that I wouldn't like to, but we're working."

"Just so you don't forget the hugs," Gram Martha-Jane teased in her soft southern way. "I'll hold you to it, you hear?" Gram's brown hair curled around her smiling face, and she looked especially nice in a white and green dress, the same soft green as her eyes. "Your mother says you're having a slumber party at your house tomorrow night."

"Yep, we are," Tricia answered.

"That should be side-splitting," Gram teased.

Tricia grinned. "I hope not!"

After they'd written *Martha-Jane Bennett* and *Jonathan Bennett* on their name tags, Tricia told them formally, "Please walk to your left, along the hallway, then go out by the pool."

"Well done," Gramp said, saluting her.

Gram smiled and waved, then started down the hallway.

"I like your gram and gramp," Becky remarked as the next guests wrote out their names.

"Me, too," Tricia agreed. "They're the best gram and gramp on this earth." The real question, she thought for the zillionth time, was why their son—her very own father—wasn't a lot more like them.

After a while, Mr. and Mrs. Exley Llewellyn arrived, an elderly couple for whom they often worked.

"What a pleasure to see you girls here," Mrs. Llewellyn said in her squawky, excited voice. She wore a white silk pantsuit that looked nice with her frazzled red hair, and Mr. Llewellyn wore a white silk suit that matched hers. Mrs. L. added, half-serious, "Now, don't you get so busy working at other people's parties that you won't have time for me."

"We'll always have time for you, Mrs. Llewellyn," Tricia promised. "After all, you gave us our party-helper start."

"Glad you remembered," Mrs. L. answered. "Some business people nowadays don't honor that sort of thing at all."

Business people?!

Tricia and Becky glanced at each other, almost laughing. Usually nothing that Mrs. L. said surprised them, she was so eccentric.

An hour later most of the guests' names were checked off, and Tricia ran her fingers down the list to be sure. When she looked up, she saw a familiar man just stepping into the entry. "Dad . . . I didn't expect you here!"

The next moment she realized he wasn't alone—and the curly black-haired woman with him was *Odette LeRoy!*

Tricia stared at them, speechless.

Dad was tall, with reddish brown hair, and handsome as ever in a yellow sand-washed silk shirt and white pants. And his hair had just been cut, making him look younger. "Cat got your tongue?" he asked.

"I—I guess so."

He grinned, but his grayish green eyes held a warning: *Don't make any trouble if you know what's good for you!*

Beside her, Becky said an uneasy, "Hello, Mr. Bennett."

He nodded. "Hello, Becky."

Tricia was glad she'd told Becky about that awful visit to L.A. and meeting Odette. At least Becky wouldn't be too shocked.

21

Odette stood with her nose in the air, probably hoping it made her appear taller. It looked to Tricia as if she tried to make up for being short and not very curvy by using lots of cosmetics: thick brownish makeup, brown eye shadow around her greenish brown eyes, both black eyebrows brushed upward, lipstick glistening in a bright red pout, and a cloud of sweet perfume wafting around her. Her sleek white sundress made her olive skin and upswept black curls look exotic, and she wore showy earrings and bracelets, and eye-catching diamond rings on her fingers. All in all, she looked and smelled e-x-p-e-n-s-i-v-e. As usual, she was twisting her car keys as if she couldn't bear being too far away from her white Corvette.

Her huge black poodle, Yvette, stood nearby, and matched her owner in corkscrew curls and snootiness. The poodle held her head high, too, as if her collar were studded with diamonds instead of rhinestones.

Suddenly an awful thought occurred to Tricia: *What will Gramp and Gram think when they see the two of them together? And what if Mom finds out?* Finally she managed, "I—I don't see your names on our list. Would you please fill out name tags?"

"Mighty cool reception, Tricia," her father replied.

"I'm working, Dad. . . ."

"I see. Aren't you supposed to be guest-friendly?"

Tricia turned a phony smile on them. "Welcome."

"Better, but not perfect," he told her. He let Odette write on their name tags, which was just as well since she hadn't spoken a single word to them.

How can I help being mad at you for leaving our family? Tricia thought. It'd been bad enough when she had visited him in L.A. and he'd been so friendly with Odette. But now . . .

everyone in Santa Rosita would know about them being to-gether!

Tricia was tempted to say, "Gramp and Gram Martha-Jane are right here at the party!" But instead, she just stared at Dad and Odette. On top of that, Yvette was snuffling at her, prob-ably picking up the scent from her cat, Butterscotch. Tricia gave the black poodle a little push with her foot, which made her back off.

Odette pressed Dad's name tag onto his shirt, her long red fingernails tapping him. "Doesn't the music sound marvel-ous?" she asked.

He nodded, a little embarrassed. "See you later, girls."

"Yeh—see you later," Tricia answered unhappily.

Odette shot her a scornful glance. "Come along, Yvette," she said to her poodle.

One thing about Odette, Tricia thought. She looked perfect for her job in a snobby Beverly Hills art gallery and her week-ends spent gambling in Las Vegas.

Once they'd disappeared around the corner, Becky shook her head. "I can't understand what he sees in her! Your mom's ten times prettier and nicer than Odette LeRoy."

"You know it."

"As for her stuck-up dog, why would she even bring a dog to a party? No one else has!"

Tricia shrugged. "Probably because her doggie psychiatrist told her Yvette needed more of a social life."

Actually, she knew the dog didn't like to be left home alone; Odette even took the poodle to work at the art gallery. Another thing, and this one made Tricia feel better: Yvette hated men as much as she hated cats, and she always wedged herself between Dad and Odette. It would almost be funny if the situation weren't so awful.

"You all right?" Becky asked.

Tricia felt tears pressing behind her eyes. She blinked hard. "Yeh. I'll be all right . . . somehow. It's Gramp and Gram that I'm worried about."

"Oooohhhh!" Becky said furiously. "I can't believe it—Odette and Yvette! Not only do I get their names mixed up, but they even look alike! They're both just overgrown, pampered puppies. Ooooohh! It makes me so mad!"

Tricia unclenched her fists. "I keep trying to remember that God loves my dad—and Odette, too . . . even if they don't know it. Gramp and Gram will think of that."

"Doesn't your father know the Lord?" Becky asked with wide-eyed amazement.

Tricia shook her head. "Afraid not. I—I've just never talked about it."

"But your grandfather—his *father*—is a minister!"

Tricia nodded. "That's what makes it all the worse. Dad pretended for a long time that he was a Christian. Mom even thought he was a believer when they were first married."

"I'm sorry," Becky said. "I'm really sorry, Trish."

Tricia bit down hard on her lower lip and nodded.

"Let's pray!" Becky said. She closed her eyes without waiting for an answer. "Heavenly Father, I pray for Tricia right now. Help her to be strong, and to be a good example to others during this trouble. We pray for her family to come together again . . . for her father to know you and . . . for even Odette to turn to you."

She'd just said "Amen" when Mrs. LeRoy stepped into the entry, surprised. "Well, praying . . . isn't that nice! No wonder

24

our guests are saying such good things about you." She headed for the open double doors. "Did everything go well?"

"Everyone was on the list," Becky said, then paused and added, "except for your granddaughter, Odette, and Mr. Bennett."

Mrs. LeRoy shot a curious look at Tricia, then closed the doors. "That's fine—I wasn't expecting them. Well, I'm sure we're done on this end now . . . and no mice so far!" She looked about nervously for a moment. "If you'll come along with me to the patio, Jess and Cara could use your help. We're ready to put food out on the buffet tables."

In the hallway, they saw Gramp and Gram Martha-Jane approaching them. "I hope you'll excuse us," Gramp said to Mrs. LeRoy. "I'm not feeling well."

"Of course," she answered with dismay. "I'm so sorry! I do hope it's nothing serious."

"I'm sure I'll be fine once I have a rest," Gramp answered.

His blue-gray eyes met Tricia's, and she could tell something was wrong with him. She clenched her fists and was glad to see a caterer had beckoned Mrs. LeRoy over to the door.

"It's not fair, Dad and Odette making you leave!"

"It's not them," Gramp said. "I truly don't feel well."

Tricia scarcely listened. "Their names weren't even on the guest list! I bet they didn't pay a cent to come here!"

"Neither did we, for that matter," Gramp told her. "We're the LeRoys' guests. Now, let's not make too much of it. It's understandable that you're angry, but if you *stay* angry, it'll make matters worse. We have to forgive your father, and Odette, too. It's the only way to be right with God."

Tricia drew a furious breath. "I know it, but I haven't

forgiven them for coming here together . . . or anything else either."

"Hard as it is, we have to," Gram Martha-Jane told her with concern.

"I'll try," Tricia mumbled. "Promise."

Tricia saw Mrs. LeRoy and Becky waiting back at the patio door for her. "I'd better go. See you Sunday."

When they arrived out on the patio, the Amazon Jazz Band was playing music with a thumping Afro-Latin rhythm, and a few of the guests were dancing the bossa nova to the music's exotic beat near the pool. Others sat at the colorful tables, smiling and enjoying the music.

Jess and Cara were hurrying around serving punch and picking up fly-away napkins. They looked relieved to see Tricia and Becky coming to help.

"Jess and Cara already have their instructions," Mrs. LeRoy said. "As soon as the guests come to the buffet, I'd like all of you to clean up the tables and put out water goblets with ice water at each place setting."

Tricia listened to the instructions, her eyes darting around the crowd. Dad and Odette sat at a table near the pool. If only she could push them in!

Before long, the caterers had carried baskets of rolls and bowls of salad, chicken, rice, and vegetables out to the buffet, and Mrs. LeRoy went out to the tables to invite guests to come up and help themselves.

"Now we spring into action!" Jess said, passing by.

For the next hour, they barely had a chance to talk to one another as they rushed about filling the water goblets and removing dirty dishes.

Thank goodness Cara was taking care of Dad's table and

the others near him, Tricia thought as she hurried along. She tried to pretend he and Odette weren't there, and once when she glanced over, Odette really was missing. Soon she was back, though, patting Yvette's head and looking phonier than ever.

Later, the Twelve Candles Club rushed about serving chocolate cheesecake and coffee, and the Amazon Jazz Band played again. It was fun to serve in time to the music. What Tricia liked best were the sounds of the gourd shaker and the beat of the snare drum.

When it began to grow dark, the band leader said, "It wouldn't be a Brazilian jazz evening without the famous Latin-American conga. Let's all get up and dance the conga."

Tricia glanced about, wondering what the conga might be, but lots of the grown-ups jumped up from their seats, delighted. Despite being elderly, the Llewellyns were some of the first on their feet, Mrs. L. cackling with excitement. In minutes, everyone was forming a line, holding on to one another's shoulders and laughing as they sang out with the music, "One-two-three, la conga! One-two-three, la conga!" On "la conga!" they kicked to one side or to the other.

"Whoa—crazy!" Tricia said, carrying dirty dessert dishes as she hurried by Cara.

"You know it," Cara answered. "Just so they don't drag us into it. It's enough to take care of two hundred guests—"

She'd no more said it than arms were grabbing out for them. "Come on, girls!" Mr. LeRoy called out merrily from the conga line, "put down your trays and let's do the conga!"

Before they knew what had happened, they were part of the line of dancers winding and kicking around the pool. Up near the buffet, Mrs. LeRoy clapped along with the music, laughing, and Tricia decided it must be okay that they had joined in the dancing. In fact, the Brazilian jazz party was fun—not at all like a dark jungly place with thumping drums and slithering snakes.

At the very moment Tricia was looking at Mrs. LeRoy, two gray mice jumped out of the bushes and scurried over the hostess's feet. She gasped in horror, then pierced the air with a loud shriek, starting screams all around her.

Next, Blackie and Calico streaked over Mrs. LeRoy's feet, racing in pursuit of the mice. From somewhere behind Tricia, Yvette barked furiously.

"Stay, Yvette!" Odette commanded. "Stay!"

Everything happened so fast that Tricia was still in the conga line, half singing out, "One, two, three—!" when Yvette bolted after the cats and crashed right into her.

Mid-kick, Tricia teetered, and at first it looked as if she'd fall into the swimming pool, but she caught her balance at the last second and instead, she fell forward, knocking Mr. LeRoy down in front of her.

Behind her, Cara had come tumbling over, and the row of conga dancers began to topple, one after another, like a row of kicking dominoes.

Luckily, everyone was laughing hilariously. "Best comedy act we've seen in a long time," a man said, and Mrs. Llewellyn cackled, "Why, it was so good, they must have planned it!"

But Odette hissed *"Really!"* at Tricia and rushed past to retrieve her black poodle.

Brushing herself off, Tricia almost hissed a "Really!" back.

"Let's get working," Cara said, trying to hide a smile.

Tricia nodded, glad that guests around them were still laughing and picking themselves up to rejoin the conga line.

She glanced toward the door and saw Odette dragging

28

Yvette by her rhinestone collar into the house.

Trouble, Tricia thought. *Odette's going to make trouble for me . . . and for the whole Twelve Candles Club.*

Nothing happened, though, and the conga dancers carried on, laughing wildly and snaking around the pool. In fact, Mrs. Llewellyn called to them, "Isn't this fun? Isn't this wonderful? It's the first time I've done the conga since our cruise to South America!"

After the conga was over and the tables were cleared, Mrs. LeRoy called out to Tricia and the others, "Girls, come eat some of this dinner from the buffet. You've been working so hard . . . and doing a good job for us, too."

"Thank you, Mrs. LeRoy," Tricia said, glad not to be blamed for the collapsing conga line.

They helped themselves to food and settled at an empty table. By the time they'd finished eating, darkness was falling and everyone was settling back in their chairs to watch the fireworks. The band played patriotic music, and Mr. LeRoy called out, "Let the fireworks begin!"

Suddenly bursts of silver and gold flared against the dark sky, followed by bright sprays of reds and greens. Burst after burst of brilliant colors crackled through the night sky while the guests ooohhhed and aaahhhed. Trying to forget about Dad and Odette, Tricia joined in, oooohing as the colors sparkled against the darkness. In the distance, fireworks from the fairgrounds made the light show even more wonderful.

All too soon, the fireworks ended and guests began to leave. After most of them had left, Odette hurried out to the patio again. "The two small French paintings have been stolen from the living room!" she announced to her grandparents. "Two of your very finest!"

"Stolen? Which ones?" Mrs. LeRoy asked, her eyes wide.

Odette told her again. "The two small French paintings from the living room!"

"How could it have happened?" Mrs. LeRoy asked, clasping a hand over her heart. "The guests were all recommended and most even sent large checks. We have all of their names—"

Suddenly Tricia knew what was coming and could only think, *Not again! Oh, Lord, please don't let anyone accuse us like Mrs. Wurtzel did at the Llewellyns'!*

But Odette LeRoy lifted her jeweled arm and pointed straight at Tricia. "As far as I could see, the only people even near the living room were those two girls who checked off names in the entry. There's one of them now—Tricia Bennett. And there's the other one from that stupid candle club."

CHAPTER

3

*T*ricia liked washing cars on Saturday mornings because it gave the Twelve Candles Club more quiet time to discuss things. No ringing phones and no yelling kids. This Saturday, as usual, they wore their grubby cut-offs and old T-shirts as they washed Mr. and Mrs. Terhune's two cars—a new white Ford and an older green Pontiac.

She wiped a soapy sponge across the driver's side of the Ford. Even though they'd begun working some time ago, her friends hadn't said a word about last night, so she decided to bring it up herself.

"What a disaster last night turned into," she said, "especially the police questioning us. I almost wished a burglar would show up, like that time at Jess's."

Jess rolled her eyes as she tugged the hose around the car, ready to rinse off the suds. "Once was enough to be eye-to-eye with a burglar, at least for me!"

Becky finished scrubbing a hubcap and looked up at Tricia. "Why didn't your dad stand up for us? Why didn't he tell them we wouldn't steal their paintings?"

"Probably because of Odette," Tricia answered unhappily. "It makes me sick to think of her. It's bad enough to have separated parents without Odious Odette in the picture."

"Odious Odette!" Cara echoed.

"You know it," Tricia agreed, remembering how the LeRoy party had ended. Two police cars had wailed up the driveway, and the officers had jumped out. They'd listened carefully to what had happened, then asked lots of questions, taken the guest list, and searched the house and grounds. Finally, they'd explained that a robbery taking place during a party with two hundred people made it almost impossible to find clues.

Even when Odette had told them about her and Becky sitting at the door, the officer in charge had said, "And how would four twelve-year-old girls get the paintings out of here?"

"They're small paintings!" Odette had snapped at the officer. "What's more, it's *your* job to find out!"

The officer had only given her a peculiar look.

Now Jess asked, "Did you tell your mom?"

Tricia nodded. "She knows we're innocent. But I didn't tell her about Dad and Odette being there last night."

She finished swishing soapy water on the front fender and decided it was a good time to end the discussion. "Okay, looks like we're done with this car. On to the next car and on to a *new* subject."

But changing the subject didn't stop her from thinking. Maybe she should have told Mom about Odette and Dad attending the party together. Oh, what she'd give to have never in her entire life even heard of Odette LeRoy!

Last night Mr. LeRoy had driven them home, and when she'd gone in, Mom had been reading a book. She'd just asked, "How'd it go?"

Tricia had told her, "Mrs. LeRoy paid us a hundred dollars, which was nice to split up!"

Mom had been impressed, and this morning she'd been too busy with Suzanne and Bryan—and making pancakes—to talk much.

"Come on, Tricia," Becky said. "Get moving! We've got lots of cars to wash this morning, and Cara and I are cleaning the Terhunes' house this afternoon, so you can get ready for your slumber party . . . *and* the special meeting of the Twelve Candles Club."

"Oh, yeah," Tricia answered. "I almost forgot."

Cara gave her a sad smile. "I can't blame you. You have a lot to think about. Believe me, none of us would like being in your place."

"I guess not," Tricia replied.

"Anyhow," Becky added, "the police don't suspect us about the paintings."

"I'm not so sure of that," Tricia answered. "Nothing would surprise me." She frowned, remembering her plans for next week. "I almost forgot that I'm trying out for the summer play Monday afternoon."

"What is it?" Cara asked.

"*Alice in Wonderland*," Tricia answered, then felt unsure. It seemed there had been talk of changing it, but someone would have told her or sent a notice. Everything seemed so confused lately because of Dad.

33

After a long moment, Jess called out, "Slumber party! Slumber party!"

"Slumber party! Slumber party!" the rest of them joined in, grinning crazily.

Probably they were doing it so she'd forget her troubles, Tricia decided. She swallowed a deep breath and, despite her sadness, had to grin herself. "Slumber party! Slumber party!" she chorused with them.

At noon, she rushed home carrying the heavy plastic basket full of dirty car-washing rags and sponges. When she reached up to unlatch the breezeway gate, rags tumbled from the tipped basket, pushing the gate open. Already she could hear Suzanne and Bryan laughing in the backyard. She flung the rags back into the basket, then headed through the breezeway of her peach-colored, two-story house.

The next moment, Chessie, their golden Labrador retriever, was licking her face, and Butterscotch, their cat, eyed her from on top of the tile drinking fountain.

"Out of here, you two," Tricia warned them. "Out of my way! I'm in no mood for having my face licked."

Chessie backed off, her brown eyes brimming with hurt feelings, and Butterscotch lifted her nose with disdain.

"Tricia, is that you?" asked her seven-year-old sister from the patio.

"It's me, all right," Tricia replied as she came around the corner.

Suzanne and their five-year-old brother, Bryan, were seated at the redwood outdoor table and began to laugh and pound crazily on the table. Just seeing them acting silly lifted Tricia's spirits a little. "Looks like you're waiting to eat."

Suzanne tucked her white paper napkin under her collar. "En-chi-la-das!" She scrunched up her face and wagged her head, making her long dark braid flop across her shoulders. "I love enchiladas!"

Bryan's reddish blond hair glistened in the sunshine as he wagged his head back and forth with her. "Me too! We love enchiladas!"

"Who'd ever guess?" Tricia asked.

Suzanne shot back, "You love them, too."

"I guess I do," Tricia agreed.

"Are you workin' more today?" Suzanne asked.

"Not this afternoon. I'm actually going to clean my room for a change."

"That's because of your slumber party," Suzanne said in her I'm-not-so-dumb voice. "You want me to help?"

Tricia shook her head. "Thanks, but no thanks. I need some quiet time this afternoon. See you crazy guys later."

Thank goodness they didn't seem too worried about Dad being gone, probably because they still didn't understand what was going on, Tricia thought. Unfortunately, she understood. Worse, she remembered hearing some awful statistics. Ninety-five percent of married people who separate never get together again. Ninety-five percent!

Lord, let my parents be in that five percent who get back together! Help Dad to see that we're really not "more trouble than we're worth." And, Lord, I pray that he would learn to love you like we do. "Amen," she murmured, letting herself in the back door.

Mom was in the kitchen just taking the glass dish of steaming enchiladas out of the oven. They were homemade enchiladas, not the usual store-bought kind, probably because they had to start watching their money. Dad was still sending them some, and Mom had inherited money, too, but they definitely didn't have as much as before Dad left. Another good reason for working in the Twelve Candles Club.

"Good timing, Tricia," Mom teased. Her lips only smiled a little, though, and her blue eyes didn't dance like they once had. "Suzanne and Bryan want to eat outside. I thought it would give us a chance to talk."

Tricia stared at her, the plastic basket of rags in her arms growing heavier. "To talk?"

"To talk," Mom echoed. She was wearing a blue T-shirt and shorts that made her eyes seem even bluer—and sadder. "You can get the washing machine started, and I'll take their lunch out to the patio table."

In the laundry room, Tricia kept her mind on getting the rags and sponges into the washing machine. Finally, she had them and the laundry soap in, and the machine started.

As she entered the kitchen and headed for their round table, she felt even more worried. "Talk about what?"

Mom slid the remaining enchiladas onto their white stoneware plates. She'd already poured two glasses of milk and set out carrot and celery sticks. "It has to do with who was at the LeRoy party last night."

Tricia swallowed and sat down on her chair. "I guess someone must have told you. Did Becky tell her mother?"

Mom shook her head, then drew a deep breath and dropped her shoulders. "Someone else told Becky's mother. Someone else who was a guest at the party. She knew it'd probably get back to me, so she called Becky's mother, knowing she was my best friend. It was a kind way for me to find out."

"Oh," Tricia answered, exhaling the breath she'd been holding.

Mom sat down on the other side of the table and folded her slender hands. "First things first, Trish. Let's pray."

"You know it," Tricia answered and bowed her head with relief.

"Dear Heavenly Father," Mom began, "thank you for so many blessings, especially my daughter, Tricia. I am so grateful for her, and for Suzanne and Bryan . . . and for this food, too. We ask now that you would give us your wisdom during our discussion. In Jesus' powerful name we pray. Amen."

"Amen," Tricia added, feeling slightly better.

She looked down at the enchiladas on her plate and, for once, didn't feel the least bit hungry.

Mom managed to smile, but only a little. "Well, it's a shame to ruin a good lunch with trouble, but I do want to ask you about Odette LeRoy and your father. Do you mind?"

Tricia felt tears press behind her eyes. "I guess not."

In the laundry room, the washing machine was groaning at its heavy load—exactly how she felt. Blinking hard to keep the tears away, she grabbed celery and carrot sticks, and piled them on her plate.

"It must have been hard for you to see Odette and your father arrive at the party," Mom began.

Tricia's voice wavered as she admitted, "Believe me, it wasn't easy."

"I'm really sorry it happened, but it did. Is there anything I should know about your visit with your father in L.A.?"

Mom looked so unhappy that a lump filled Tricia's throat. "I didn't want to be the one to tell you. I just hoped that you'd never ever find out. But since they came to her grandparents' party together, I guess I should tell."

Tricia drew a deep breath. "Anyhow, they live in the same condo complex and . . . well, they seemed a little too friendly when I visited. Odette even went out to lunch and dinner with Dad and me. She'd just broken up with someone else, and it sounded to me like she thought he—the other man—was going to marry her."

"So she's hurting, too," Mom remarked thoughtfully.

"She acted mad about him not marrying her, all right. About as mad as could be and complained about him."

"Poor thing," Mom said. "I almost feel sorry for her."

"Not me!"

Mom raised her brows. "I heard that Gram and Gramp Bennett were at the LeRoy party, too, and that they left early."

"He wasn't feeling well," Tricia explained. "I've thought over and over about his leaving early, and I know he wouldn't lie about not feeling well . . . or anything else, either."

"Hmmmm," Mom said, picking up a forkful of enchiladas and taking a thoughtful bite. "In today's selection of my devotional book, I read about God's promise that we can have victory even during the difficult times. I believe that promise, and Trish, I am going to trust God that this will someday be a victory."

"You really think God will get us through this?" Tricia asked.

"If we trust Him entirely," Mom said. "And since there's nothing else I can think of to do myself, trusting Him is exactly what I intend to do!"

"Then . . . I'll do it, too," Tricia decided. She sighed. "First, though, I guess I'd better forgive Dad and Odette."

Mom nodded with certainty. "Good. I have already, and I

expect I'll have to do it every single time I think of them for some time to come."

"I guess so," Tricia answered. "Gramp reminded me that I should, too."

"And you're going to have to forgive whoever stole the paintings and caused the blame to come on you girls."

"I guess so," Tricia agreed unhappily.

She bowed her head and said quietly, "Lord, I do forgive Dad and Odette in every way possible, and I ask that your love would come into my heart for them. Help Mom and me to trust you in this mess. And please help the police find the stolen paintings and get the blame off of us. Amen."

Tricia opened her eyes and straightened up.

"Good," Mom said. "I'm really proud of you, Trish."

The washing machine whirred in the laundry room, and nothing seemed very different. In fact, nothing had changed except Mom's expression. Instead of the sadness, she looked really hopeful.

"One other thing," Mom said. "How you deal with this problem is important for your friends' sakes. Jess and Cara have just begun coming to church and Becky's only been a Christian for two years. They will be watching to see how you handle this."

"I hadn't thought of that. . . ."

"On a happier note, I hear something hilarious happened at the party," Mom said, "but Becky's mother was interrupted and never got around to telling me what it was."

"Now that you mention it, something funny did happen," Tricia replied. "When we were all out on the patio and dinner was over, people were dancing the conga. In the middle of it, two mice ran across Mrs. LeRoy's feet, and her cats were chasing right after them. Then Odette's poodle, Yvette, started chasing the cats, and Yvette knocked me down, along with half of the conga line."

Mom almost laughed. "You're kidding! You mean the mice actually ran onto the patio with all of the people there?"

Despite everything, Tricia had to grin. "I'm not kidding. The cats drove the mice out of the bushes. The funniest part, though, was the conga line toppling all around us, people falling down one after another like dominoes. I wish Cara had made one of her videos of that sight!"

"So do I!" Mom said with a smile. "You girls sure do get into peculiar situations."

Tricia laughed. "Now that I'm not in the middle of the mess, it seems lots funnier."

"I can imagine!" Mom said. After a moment, she added thoughtfully, "Maybe someday the problems we're going through now will seem less troublesome, too." She gave Tricia a smile that reached all the way into her blue eyes. "You know, I feel better. There's nothing like laughter to cure the blues."

Tricia nodded. "I feel better, too." Suddenly her stomach sent up a hunger pang. "Whoa—it's even made me hungry!" She took up a bit of enchilada on her fork and eyed it fiercely. "Look out, enchilada! Here come the scary mouth and sharp teeth of Tricia Bennett!"

Look out, trouble, too! she decided as she bit in. It was impossible for her to do anything to fix their family now, but God could do it. *He can-can-can-can do it!*

CHAPTER

4

*L*ater that afternoon, Tricia was upstairs in her room when she heard her friends coming up the driveway. "Slumber party! Slumber party!" they chanted as they trooped toward her house.

I am not-not-not going to think about Dad and Odette, or about the stolen paintings, Tricia promised herself. She glanced down from her open window at Jess, Cara, and Becky carrying their sleeping bags and other stuff. Until yesterday, only Becky had known about Dad and Odette, but now all of them knew. This morning, at the car-washing, they'd been busy, but slumber parties were when they talked about private things. What if they started to ask questions? Or worse, what if they acted sorry for her!

"Be right down!" she called down through the window.

She cast a quick look around her bedroom. It looked like an indoor garden with its moss green carpeting, white wicker furniture, and pots of trailing grape ivy. Puffy white comforters and pillows on the twin beds were sprinkled with tiny green leaves and peach-colored flowers. Green-and-white-checkered skirts on the beds and ruffles around the pillows added to the garden theme. A matching green and white cushion covered the window seat that overlooked the pepper trees along the street.

Despite her troubles, seeing the room look so nice made her feel better. "All right!" she called out and headed for her bedroom door. So what if she'd cried about her family's problems this afternoon. She was *not* going to think about Dad and Odette anymore today.

Besides, no one could stay interested in a phoney-baloney baby doll like Odette for long. *Wake up, Dad!* she thought.

Racing down the stairs, she recited good and loud, "How do you like to go up in a swing, up in the air so blue? Oh, I do think it the pleasantest thing ever a child can do! Up in the air and over the walls, till I can see so wide—"

She was just at the "Till I look down on the garden green, down on the roof so brown—" when she threw the door open and finished the poem to her friends with, "—up in the air I go flying again, up in the air and down!"

"You wacko!" Becky laughed.

"Wacko, wacko, wacko!" Jess and Cara chorused, laughing.

Tricia raised her chin and grinned. "Up in the air I go flying again, up in the air and down!"

Jess shook her head. "Where'd you learn that stuff, anyhow?"

"From the old poetry books Gram Martha-Jane gave me," Tricia answered. "Now, up in the air to my room!"

42

Becky gave a hopeless shake of her head, then said in a comical voice, "Don't mind if we do."

Tricia laughed, her voice cracking a little. She panicked. If she wasn't careful, they'd suspect how upset she was. Starting up the stairs, she flung out the words again, "Up in the air I go flying again—"

They all joined in with her, "Up in the air and down!" then laughed wildly.

"You're going to make all of us wacko!" Jess exclaimed.

"We already are," Becky announced.

Cara only shook her head and said a "You know it."

As they arrived in her room, Tricia felt better. They'd have a fun time tonight, and she'd be all right, too.

Her friends dropped their sleeping bags and overnight bags on the floor by her louvered closet doors. Becky and Cara sat down on the window seat, and Jess plopped down on the floor.

Tricia sat on her twin bed, the nearest to the window seat. "Whoa, we're all wearing white again!"

"It's getting to be our uniform," Becky answered. "Anyhow, it's nice in the summer."

Jess crawled across the carpet to the pile of overnight bags. She zipped hers open, then pulled out a pencil, her daily planner, and a sheet of paper. "Don't forget, this is supposed to be a special meeting of the Twelve Candles Club, too. Let's get it over with. I've got five more phone calls for jobs. Did you all bring your daily planners?"

Cara and Becky got theirs from the overnight bags, and Tricia grabbed hers from the row of books against the back of her white wicker desk.

"Are we ever without these anymore?" Cara asked. "I didn't think we'd be working so much when we got started."

43

"You're getting rich, aren't you?" Jess asked as she smoothed out the wrinkles on the paper.

"Not exactly rich," Cara replied. "But I have lots more money than I ever dreamed I'd have this summer."

Tricia flipped through her daily planner to the fifth of July. "I'm all set," she announced.

"This meeting of the Twelve Candles Club will now come to order," Becky announced in her most formal voice. She even straightened her spine as she sat on the window-seat cushion. "Will the secretary, Cara Hernandez, please read the minutes?"

Cara rolled her brown eyes at the ceiling and opened her notebook.

"Come on!" Jess said, laughing at Becky. "For someone who couldn't remember how to conduct a meeting just one month ago, you sure do act presidential now."

"If the secretary would please read the minutes of the last meeting—" Becky repeated, trying not to grin.

Tricia put a hand to her mouth to keep from smiling at her best friend. "Presidential" was exactly the word for her now at meetings.

"At the last meeting of the Twelve Candles Club," Cara read from her notebook, "we discussed the jobs already offered for the month of July and decided who would take what. We also decided to continue Morning Fun for Kids on Monday, Wednesday, and Friday mornings at Tricia's house. Even though it's hard work to take care of so many little kids, it helps us to get extra baby-sitting and party-helper jobs. . . ."

What would she have done if the Twelve Candles Club hadn't started? Tricia asked herself. Probably mope and cry all summer long. If it weren't for the club, it'd be the most awful summer of her life.

She only half heard Cara read the rest of the minutes about who'd taken which job. Anyhow, she already remembered the party-helper job at the Llewellyns' the last Saturday of the month and Chelsea Sanderson's sixth birthday party on Thursday. And she knew the steady jobs: cleaning for Mrs. Llewellyn on Thursday mornings until her cleaning lady was well, and for Mrs. O'Lone, who lived over by the ocean, on Tuesday mornings.

"Come in, Tricia Ellen Bennett!" Becky announced as if she were paging planet Mars for the zillionth time. "Come in, Tricia Ellen Bennett! Are you here or there?"

"Sorry," Tricia apologized. She noticed that even Jess, doing her leg stretches against the wall, was watching her.

"It's time for you to read the treasurer's report."

"Sorry," she said again, "I was thinking about something else." She waited for someone to make a stupid remark, but instead, they were eyeing her with real concern. She looked down quickly and opened her green notebook to the last entry. "Treasurer's Report," she read, keeping her voice light. "The Twelve Candles Club has $3.39 in the treasury. All bills are paid. Respectfully submitted, Patricia Ellen Bennett."

"Thank you," Becky said. "Any comments?"

"Yep," Tricia answered, beginning to feel more confident. "We'd better each pay in two dollars so there's enough money to buy juice, raisin packs, and graham crackers for next week. Snacks cost a lot."

"Let's all pay in five dollars each so we don't have to always be collecting," Jess said. "Ooops! I mean, I make a motion that we each pay five dollars into the treasury."

45

"I second the motion," Cara added.

Becky drew a breath. "It's been moved and seconded that we each pay in five dollars."

Everyone got up and dug their wallets out of their overnight bags while Becky finished with the formalities.

As they paid up, Tricia entered their names in the day's treasurer's report. When they finished, she announced, "Madame President, all members are paid up. I hereby report that we now have $23.39 in the treasury of the Twelve Candles Club."

"Whoa, that's the most ever!" Cara said.

Jess was back into leg-stretching position against the wall. "That should keep Treasurer Tricia off our backs for a week or so."

Tricia managed a Cheshire cat smile at them. "Let's hope so! But treats for kids are important."

"You know it," Cara said. "It's the *only* time they're ever quiet at Morning Fun for Kids, except maybe for moments during the Magic Carpet rides!"

"Which reminds me," Tricia said, "don't forget to wear western clothes Monday morning for Cowboy Day. Mom's making red bandanas for the kids to wear around their necks."

"Whoa, we can wear the western stuff Mrs. Llewellyn gave us to wear for her first party!" Jess exclaimed. "Hi-ho, cowboy!"

"Only let's wear them with white Tees and blue jeans," Becky suggested.

"Cut-offs for me," Jess said. "They're lots better for gymnastics."

"Should we have something special to eat?" Tricia asked, since she was in charge of buying snacks.

"Yeh!" Jess said. "Why not trail mix?"

"Trail mix?" Cara echoed, perplexed.

"Sure," Jess answered. "Cowboys riding out on the trail. There's even a cowboy song, 'Happy Trails to You.' Don't tell me you've never heard it!"

"Okay, okay, I've got it," Cara said.

Everyone agreed on serving trail mix, even though it'd probably be more expensive than their usual graham crackers.

"What do cowboys drink?" Jess asked.

"Coffee . . . lots of coffee," Tricia answered. "That's what the cowboys drank when we went to that dude ranch in Arizona last summer."

"Better stay with the orange juice," Becky said. "Trail mix and orange juice."

"You know, we could do cowboy birthday parties, too," Cara suggested. "Maybe if the kids have already had one of our clown parties, they'd like a cowboy party instead."

Suddenly, Tricia remembered her try-out for *Alice in Wonderland* Monday afternoon. "We've already got enough to do."

"We can worry about cowboy parties *next* summer," Becky put in, "though you might want to make a note of it in the minutes of the meeting."

Finally the meeting turned to old business, then to new business. "How about dog-sitting?" Jess asked them as she stretched a leg behind her. "Mrs. LeRoy called this afternoon to see if we'd do it."

No one answered for a moment, then Cara asked, "Why not? It's probably easier than baby-sitting. I didn't know they had a dog, though."

"It's not theirs," Jess answered. "It's Odious Odette's black poodle."

Tricia felt a surge of indignation. "Why would she ask us to dog-sit Odette's dog? She lives in L.A.!"

"Because Odette's taking some vacation here in Santa Rosita at her grandparents' house," Jess explained. "That's why she was at the party last night. She'll be going to the beach and shopping, and poor Yvette can't go along. Mrs. LeRoy said Yvette causes too much trouble if she's left alone in their house."

Tricia recalled the stories Odette had told Dad and her about Yvette going wild in her condo when she was left alone—chewing up the carpet and, one time, jumping over the second-floor balcony into the bushes. "I guess so," she said. "She'd tear up the whole house. She's probably like Odette . . . needs a lot of watching!"

Everyone smiled a little.

"Do you mind if we dog-sit Odette?" Becky asked. Suddenly her face turned red and she clapped a hand to her forehead. "I mean Yvette? I get their names mixed up!"

Tricia giggled out loud, and the rest of them laughed, too, glancing uneasily at Tricia.

"Really!" Jess exclaimed. "They do kinda look like twinnies with that black curly hair, don't they? Maybe we should buy Odette a rhinestone collar so we can't tell them apart at all!"

Tricia felt a little mean, but the thought of Odious Odette in a dog collar was just too funny. "I almost feel sorry for Yvette. She probably learned her snooty manners—not to mention crashing into people and knocking down a whole conga line—from her mistress. Guess the poor pooch can't help it if insanity runs in the family. But I don't want to dog-sit her, that's for sure." She shuddered. "Yuck!"

"They can leave her with the maid and gardener some of the time," Jess explained. "I told Mrs. LeRoy about our regular jobs, and she said she'd take whatever time we're available. She's paying five dollars an hour, like last night, and she'll send someone to pick up and bring the dog-sitter home."

Everyone looked at each other for a minute. Finally Becky said, "I don't have any cards or pizza invitations to make this week. If you don't mind, Tricia, I could really . . . use the money."

Tricia knew the extra money would help her best friend's family, which was why they'd started the Twelve Candles Club anyhow. "Go ahead," she told her. "I just hope Odette doesn't bite you!"

They all laughed uneasily, knowing she'd confused their names on purpose.

Why, oh, why didn't Odious Odette and her stupid poodle just stay in L.A. and out of her family's life? Tricia thought angrily. Just when she'd almost forgotten her troubles, they had to come up again now at her slumber party!

Becky looked eager to change the subject. "Any other jobs or new business?"

"Four other jobs," Jess replied. "All baby-sitting."

"Count me in," Tricia told her. Maybe Mom would need money before long, too. She'd inherited some from her grandmother, but if Dad stopped sending money, they might have financial troubles like Becky's family.

Jess smoothed out the wrinkled paper again. "Two Sunday night baby-sitting jobs. The Stallings have asked for Cara at six o'clock, as usual."

"I'll take it," Cara said.

Jess read from the wrinkled paper. "And ummmm . . . yeh,

Sunday . . . a new family that just moved into Santa Rosita Estates, the Wilheits, heard about us from Mrs. Davis. They've got a baby and a three-year-old girl."

"How about you, Jess?" Becky asked.

Jess lifted her shoulders. "Believe it or not, I'm going to a Sunday night praise and worship service with Dad and Jordan at the church, so I'm busy."

"Glad to hear it," Tricia said, since Jess and Cara had only recently begun to attend Santa Rosita Community Church. "I bet you'll like it a lot."

"I hope so," Jess answered, not sounding certain.

"And I'm baby-sitting Amanda," Becky put in. "Mom's got a date with Mr. Bradshaw *again*."

"Again?" everyone asked.

Becky laughed. "Again! Only tonight they're not taking three kids with them, like last night at the fair."

When everyone quieted, Tricia said, "I'll take the Wilheit job. Anyhow, I like taking care of babies."

"Not me!" Jess announced. "Not with diapers and bottles and burping and stuff. You're a weird one, Tricia."

"You know it," Tricia agreed, then wrote down all of the job details.

Jess and Becky took the other two baby-sitting jobs, and finally Becky announced, "The next meeting will be Monday afternoon at four o'clock, as usual. This special meeting of the Twelve Candles Club is now adjourned."

"So be it," Tricia pronounced like a final amen.

Minutes later, Suzanne knocked at the door. She said in a hushed tone, "Mom says I should tell you to come outside for dinner!"

"Thanks—we'll be right there," Tricia answered. She

hadn't heard Suzanne come up the stairs and wondered how long she'd been snooping. "You can go down now, Suzanne."

Fortunately, on the way downstairs and through the house, none of her friends mentioned that "odious person." When they arrived outside on the back patio, though, Jess and Cara eyed Mom as if she might have been crying.

Instead, Mom's blue eyes sparkled with pleasure. "It's so nice to see you girls working with such enthusiasm this summer," she said as she turned the burgers on the grill. "I'm proud of you, and the Lord must be, too."

Tricia glanced at Jess and Cara, who weren't used to religious talk in their families. They both nodded a bit nervously. Becky was used to it—living next door and her mother being Mom's best friend.

Mom turned the last hamburger and pressed it down against the grill, making the fat sizzle on the charcoal. "As soon as this side is cooked, I'm taking our hamburgers, and Suzanne, Bryan, and I are having potluck over at Becky's house," she said as the meat sizzled. "That way I'll be next door if you need me, but you'll have the house to yourselves for a while."

"Thanks, Mom," Tricia said. She wasn't too surprised, though, since Mom was usually thoughtful.

She noticed that Suzanne and Bryan looked slighted. It was nice to have them for a little brother and sister, but sometimes it was a relief not to have them snooping around.

Finally they left, and Tricia sat on a bench at the redwood table with her friends. Each paper plate held a burger, and bowls of olives, carrot sticks, and homemade potato salad stood in the middle of the table.

"Should we hold hands and pray?" Tricia suggested.

They'd never done it before, but now that Jess and Cara were going to church, too, it seemed like a good idea.

"Why not?" Jess asked, holding out her hands.

Cara looked uneasy, but Tricia grabbed for her hand and Becky's, and began. "Dear Heavenly Father, thanks for this day and for this food . . . and for the fun time our club always has together. Amen."

"Amen," Becky added.

"And amen!" Tricia pronounced with a joyous finality.

Even Cara was smiling.

Grinning, Tricia spread mustard, ketchup, and mayonnaise on a bun, centered a meat patty and a tomato slice on one side, and slapped it together. It barely fit into her mouth, but it tasted as wonderful as it felt to pray with friends.

"Whoa, you forgot the potato salad!" Becky said.

"So I did," Tricia answered, suddenly feeling wild and wacko. "Fling some onto my plate."

Jess sat across the table, but she dug the big serving spoon into the potato salad and flung it toward Tricia, where it landed on her plate with a splat.

"Hey, now me!" Becky laughed.

They were crazily flinging potato salad onto one another's plates when the outdoor phone near the kitchen rang. "Scusa me," Tricia said and grabbed it.

"Hello, Bennetts' residence—"

"Hi, Tricia," her father said. "How are you?"

She darted a glance at her friends and was glad to see they weren't listening. "Fine," she answered, not sounding very friendly.

"I need to talk to your mother," he said, his voice stiffer, too.

She almost told him Mom was next door at the Hamiltons, but stopped herself. "She's . . . she's out tonight."

His voice filled with suspicion. "Is she . . . is she out on a date?"

Tricia clenched her fists and decided not to answer at all. If Mom *were* out on a date, it wouldn't be any of his business! He was the one who'd left them! Worse, he was the one who was dating!

He cleared his voice. "Never mind. I need to pick up some papers at the house—"

"You'll have to ask her," she said, furious to be drawn into his problems. "I'm having a slumber party right now!"

"Your club?" he asked.

"Yes, the Twelve Candles Club!"

"You know, young lady, you're sounding way too important now that you're in that club—"

"I am not!" she interrupted.

"You are. If you don't watch yourself, Tricia, you'll have to give up that club."

"I will not give up the club!" she flared. "You're the one who's making all the—" She almost said "trouble" but something stopped her. "I'm sorry, Dad," she half whispered. "I'm sorry I was so rude!"

"I'm glad to hear it," he muttered, angry. "I'll call your mother later."

"Thanks," Tricia answered faintly.

She said louder, "Thanks, Dad," but he'd already hung up.

She'd no more than put her phone down than tears burst to her eyes. Knowing her friends were watching, she whirled away. Just minutes ago, she'd made a big show of leading them in prayer—and now she'd almost let the Lord down! As for quitting the Twelve Candles Club, she couldn't . . . she just couldn't! It'd been stupid of her to lose her temper and make Dad turn against the club.

She sent up a desperate prayer. *Oh, Lord, I'm so confused! If my dad is being such a jerk, do I still have to honor him? And if so, what should I honor? His yucky girlfriend? I hate him for making our lives such a mess! And I hate myself for hating him! What am I supposed to do?*

CHAPTER

5

When Tricia turned back, her friends sitting at the table looked almost as miserable as she felt. The Twelve Candles Club had been the most exciting and wonderful thing they'd ever had going, and now her anger had turned Dad against it.

The silence between them lasted so long that she finally said, "I lost my temper. I must have sounded as nasty as Odette."

Jess finished chewing a mouthful of hamburger. "You think he'd really make you give up the club?"

Tricia shrugged. "I sure hope not."

"The club wouldn't be any good without you," Becky said. "One of the main reasons Morning Fun for Kids is doing so well is your Magic Carpet rides, and you're the one who thought up clowning for kids' birthday parties. No way can we do them without you!"

"Let's not even think about it," Tricia answered. "Come

on, let's eat the burgers before they get cold. There's ice cream in the freezer, too. Not to mention chocolate sauce and nuts and other topping stuff."

"Yum!" Cara said, pretending nothing had gone wrong.

"Yeh, yum!" Jess echoed. "This burger is good, too!"

Tricia had scarcely tasted her first bite when she felt a strong but insistent urge to call her father back. It was the still, small voice kind of urge that God spoke in—not the rash, reckless, and almost ranting urge that came from His enemy's side. "Guess I'd better go in and call Dad to tell him how sorry I really am," she decided aloud. "Trouble is, I don't know where he phoned from."

"Was he in town?" Becky asked.

"He must have been, since he wanted to stop by for some papers," Tricia replied. "Maybe he's at Gramp and Gram Martha-Jane's house, since it's only forty-five minutes away. One time he stayed there because it's closer than Los Angeles." Another thought hit, and this one caused a sickening lump to fill her throat. *Maybe he is with Odette LeRoy at her grandparents' house.*

"Better call him now, before it's too late," Becky suggested. "If you don't, he might get madder yet, and then you'd really be in t-r-o-u-b-l-e."

"I guess so," Tricia answered, making herself get up and go into the house.

At the kitchen phone, she looked at the automatic dial list, then pressed the button for Gramp and Gram's phone. She drew a deep breath, listening to the faraway ringing at their house. *One ring . . . two . . . three . . . four . . .*

Gramp's warm voice came onto his answering machine with

"I'm sorry, we can't come to the phone now, but we'll be pleased to answer your call—"

Tricia hung up unhappily. Now she'd have to call the LeRoy estate. She quickly got out the phone book, hunted up their number, and dialed it before she lost her nerve.

As it rang, she heard her friends having a fine time outside and wished she could be there with them. *Lord, help me to be more loving to Dad*—she began.

"Hello, the LeRoy residence," Odette answered on the other end of the line.

"Hello," Tricia said. "It's Tricia Bennett. I . . . was wondering if my father is there. He just phoned." Odette didn't answer, and Tricia put in a fast, "I'm calling to ask his forgiveness—"

"One moment, please," Odette replied in a frosty voice. She must have put her hand over the phone, but Tricia could hear a muffled but haughty, "It's your daughter for you."

"Hello?" Dad said a moment later, not sounding at all happy about her phoning him there.

"Hi, Dad," Tricia answered. "I—I called to ask your forgiveness for being so nasty when you called." She gulped, then said, "Will you forgive me, Dad? I'm really sorry."

His voice softened. "Since you're asking so nicely, I don't have much choice. Is your mother back yet?"

"No, she isn't. Can . . . may I take a message for her?"

"I'll phone her later. And thanks for calling, Tricia. It couldn't have been easy for you."

"No, but . . . I love you, Dad."

He hesitated, then said, "I love you, too, kiddo. And Suzanne and Bryan too. You tell 'em. Thanks for calling."

This time she hung up the phone with relief. He might be

with Odette at the LeRoys' house, but he still loved his family. Maybe her phone call would make a difference to him and even to Odette, if she'd overheard them.

Outside, her friends were finishing their burgers. "How'd it go?" Becky asked her.

Tricia slid onto the bench again. "Not perfect, but I feel better about it. God knew what He was doing when He told us to forgive others."

"I guess so," Jess answered, "not that I know so much about it yet."

"Hey!—let's forget about bad stuff now and have some fun," Tricia told them. "How about doing our world-famous klutz act to cheer us up?"

They leapt to their feet, then starting to giggle, lined up on the patio. Crossing their eyes and turning their feet inward, they stumbled about wildly. "Klutz! Klutz! Klutz!" they called out, crazy as usual. Next, they bent over and wagged their arms back and forth like gorillas.

They all laughed, then Becky, who was the klutziest of them anyhow, began it again. "Klutz! Klutz! Klutz! Klutz!"

The nosey Coobler boys next door hung their heads over the fence. "What are you crazy girls up to?" nine-year-old Cody asked them.

"Let's get 'em!" Tricia said, joining in. Bending over, she wagged her arms back and forth with her friends and yelled, "Klutz . . . klutz . . . klutz . . ."

"It's the planet of the apes!" Cody's ten-year-old brother shouted, then they both laughed nervously.

"Catch 'em!" Jess yelled. "Let's catch those Coobler kids! Get your video camera, Cara, and we'll have evidence of them spying. You can sell it to the TV stations, too! Klutz! Klutz! Klutz!"

They klutzed over to the fence like gorillas, and Cody and Doug Coobler yelled, "Monsters! Let's get out of here!"

Becky added in a spooky voice, "L-e-t's g-e-t t-h-o-s-e C-o-o-b-l-e-r k-i-d-s a-n-d t-u-r-n 'e-m i-n-t-o f-r-e-n-c-h-f-r-i-e-d b-r-o-c-c-o-l-i!"

"S-p-i-n-a-c-h!" Cara yelled.

"R-u-t-a-b-a-g-a-s!" Jess shouted. She took a running leap that looked as if it would catapult her over the fence at the Coobler boys.

"You're crazy!" one of the boys yelled as they ran for their back door.

"You know it!" Tricia shouted as they ran in.

"That should take care of them for now," Jess said.

"I didn't bring the video camera," Cara told them.

"I know it and you know it," Jess said, "but they didn't know it. You think we really scared them?"

Tricia laughed. "Maybe they think we're really wacko!"

Mom's voice came from over the fence on the other side of the yard. "It wouldn't surprise me a bit!"

And there were Becky's mom—and Amanda, Suzanne, and Bryan, who were probably standing on a bench—looking over the fence, too, and laughing like anything.

"Let's get 'em!" Jess yelled, and the TCC klutzed their way over to them, making the kids shriek with laughter and run too.

When they'd gotten rid of their audiences, Jess announced, "Bring on dessert for the monsters!"

That night, when they got into their sleeping bags in her room, they laughed as much as ever—mostly at whose feet were going to be by whose nose as they slept. And then, when Jess fell asleep, they hid her undies in the freezer.

It was a good slumber party, Tricia thought as she tried to go to sleep. In the morning, Jess would probably yell, "You idiots!" when she found her frozen undies. They'd tell her that's what she got for snoring, even if she didn't snore much.

Just before nine o'clock the next morning, Mom drove them in the minivan through the hazy sunshine to Santa Rosita Community Church. She'd made Suzanne and Bryan sit in the front seat with her, to keep them from pestering Tricia and her friends.

Mom was always generous about opening up their house for slumber parties, but she had made it clear that it was no excuse for missing church. Tricia and her friends felt a little groggy, but they'd have naps this afternoon.

Beside Tricia in the middle seat, Becky said with a smile, "We had a great time last night."

"Glad to hear it," Tricia answered. "I did, too." She'd almost forgotten about Dad's phone call until earlier this morning when the phone had begun to ring. Mom had taken the call in her bedroom, and she was quieter than usual, but Tricia decided not to think about it.

Anyhow, all of the Twelve Candles Club looked nice in new sundresses and white sandals, since now they could all buy their own clothes. Mom had told them they looked like summer flowers in their sundresses: Cara in a flowery peach-colored print, Jess in all white, Becky in her blue with the tiny white butterflies, and Tricia in green with white swirls.

"Petunias?" Cara asked.

Tricia's mom smiled back at them in the rearview mirror. "No, more like snapdragons."

Tricia wondered if that referred to her having been snappy last night with Dad, but decided not to ask. "Here we are!" she announced as they pulled into the church parking lot. Despite all of her family troubles, it was a good feeling for her friends to be here with her.

The white stucco buildings of Santa Rosita Community Church were topped by red tile roofs and surrounded by lots of trees, and red geraniums bloomed around the bright green lawn. Already, cars jammed the parking lot, and a man waved them to the overflow lot, where there were still a few empty spaces.

Finally, Mom parked the minivan between two cars, and they all got out on the crunchy gravel. Tricia noticed that Mom wore her old blue summer dress that matched her eyes, and she looked especially beautiful. It seemed a shame Dad couldn't compare her to Odious Odette now. Mom was the out-and-out winner in every way.

"It's such a joy to see you girls coming to church together," Mom said to them.

Tricia glanced at Jess and Cara, wondering how they'd take the remark. Jess grinned with pleasure, but Cara, who was shy anyhow, hunched her shoulders a little as if she were closing in on herself. It seemed forever ago, but it'd only been last week that she'd had a real disaster at the youth group's beach party.

They headed through the parked cars on the crunchy gravel, Mom herding Suzanne and Bryan ahead of her. "I'll take these two today," she offered.

"Thanks," Tricia answered, glad to be relieved of her usual

61

duty. Not that she didn't like her brother and sister—usually.

"See you later!" Mom told them.

Tricia gave a wave with her friends, and they took off for the red-tile-roofed buildings. "Whew! On our own!" she said with a laugh, and they all grinned with her.

It was easy to see that Jess and Cara still felt unsure about where to go, and Tricia decided it was best to make them—and her—feel more comfortable. Arms outstretched, she balanced along as if she were a tightrope walker, which was exactly how she felt lately about Dad, anyhow. "Vroommmmm . . . vroommmm . . . this way!" she called out to them, careening this way and that. "This is the way, walk ye in it!"

Jess shook her head hopelessly. "Where'd you get *that* saying, anyhow?"

It had just popped into her head, Tricia realized. She hadn't even thought where it'd come from, but now that she remembered, it made her feel peculiar to have spoken the words so flippantly.

"From the Bible," she replied. "Come to think of it, walking a tightrope is a little like following Jesus sometimes. You get behind Him, following along, and He takes you right through exciting, even i-m-p-o-s-s-i-b-l-e adventures. At least that's what Gramp says. Gram Martha-Jane does, too."

The words came to her again, but this time she didn't say them aloud: *This is the way, walk ye in it.* They seemed almost like a calming reminder for her to follow Him, and to not worry too much about what was going on all around her.

Looking up, she realized that people were staring at her as she pretended to tightrope walk along the sidewalk. She put her arms down.

They arrived at their pale green classroom, and the folding

chairs were already filling with kids—most of them older, like eighth and ninth graders. "Here we are," she announced to her friends, as if they didn't know it.

In front of the classroom, Bear, the youth minister, was talking to some of the older kids as he settled down on a chair with his guitar. He was short and stocky with broad shoulders, and looked a little like a teddy bear.

The older kids were heading for the chairs now, and Bear gave the rest of them a wave and a good smile. "Welcome, all," he said in his nice deep voice.

"Hey, Bear!" Tricia replied with the others, since she really liked him. Maybe she could ask him what to do about her family problems and just how she was supposed to honor her father now. Maybe Bear would have an answer. On the other hand, it might be best to ask someone older like Gramp and Gram Martha-Jane. Maybe she should call them when she was alone.

Becky grabbed four papers and handed them around. "Here're the song sheets and other handouts."

Finally everyone was settled, and Bear plunked out a few chords on his guitar and then beamed at them. "Let everything that has breath praise the Lord! Let's start praising Him with 'Our God Is an Awesome God.' "

As he started playing the song, Tricia sang out with the rest of them, throwing her heart and spirit into praising the God who reigned from heaven "with wisdom, power, and love."

"Love never fails," Bear told them before starting the next praise song.

The words pierced Tricia's head and heart: L-o-v-e n-e-v-e-r f-a-i-l-s. *Lord, help me have that kind of love for my earthly father.*

When they'd finished singing, she was beginning to feel joyous and loving again. God is in control of me if I'll let Him be, she told herself.

Bear put down his guitar. "Last Sunday we had the first five of the Ten Commandments. Anyone remember what His commandments are for?"

"They're God's rules to keep us from hurting ourselves and others," someone volunteered.

"They help us to live happier, more peaceful lives," Becky added, "because we don't get all mixed up with . . . umm . . . trouble and guilt."

"Right," Bear replied. "In fact, right on!" He reached for his handouts and flipped through the pages. "This morning, we'll read the last five commandments through, then talk about them. He looked out at the kids. "Hmmm, let's see . . . Tricia Bennett, would you please read the Fifth Commandment from the handouts?"

"Sure." Tricia hunted through the handout pages. "Here it is. Fifth Commandment. . . ."

She almost gasped to see what it was. Why had Bear chosen her to read it? Why? He didn't know her problems. . . . Did he?

Finally she forced herself to read, "Honor your father and your mother, as the Lord your God has commanded you, so that you may live long and that it may go well with you in the land the Lord your God is giving you."

The other commandments passed like a blur through her mind: "You shall not commit murder . . . not commit adultery . . . not steal . . . not give false testimony against your neighbor . . . not covet. . . ."

Why had Bear chosen her to read the commandment about

honoring her father and mother? Was God using Bear to warn her?

"What if your mother or father is into something bad?" someone asked. "You know, something dishonorable."

Tricia sat stunned in her chair. Other kids must have the very same problems!

Bear raised his eyebrows and drew a thoughtful breath. "The answer is a conditional yes," he said. "A parent's position deserves respect because God has placed her or him in authority over the kids. But if Mom or Dad is acting in an ungodly way, then you have to find ways to honor them and still honor God. For example, if a father has changed from a godly to an ungodly man, you'll have to try to honor his wishes as he *would have* expressed them if he were his 'normal' self."

"I don't understand . . . exactly," said someone in the rear of the room.

"In other words," Bear answered, "you should be obedient to what the 'good side' of that father would probably have told you before. Honor a parent the very best you can without being ungodly. And pray a lot about it. Why don't all of us pray now . . . for our own parents and for other kids' parents?"

Everyone else had been as interested in what Bear was saying as she was, Tricia noticed as she bowed her head. What's more, she suddenly realized that God had answered her prayers about what to do, through Bear's guidance.

God, she prayed, *thanks for the help. But now you're going to have to help me honor my father!*

CHAPTER

6

Tricia caught a last glance at herself in the mirror: red cowgirl hat tipped back, red bandana over a white T-shirt, blue jeans, and tan cowboy boots. She looked perfect for Morning Fun for Kids' Cowboy Day; in fact, she looked as if nothing in her life were wrong.

Feeling a lump under her left cowboy boot, she leaned over to look under it. Ufff! A blob of dried-up chewing gum. Exactly what she felt like in Dad's life now, she grouched. Tricia pried off the gum and tossed it into the wastebasket, just like Dad was trying to do to them.

No, I will not think about it! she told herself. *God is in charge.*

She grabbed her rope lariat from the floor of her closet. Even with God in charge, she felt like quitting the Twelve Candles Club and not even trying out for Alice this afternoon. Most of all, she felt like hiding from her troubles and never being brave again.

But then she remembered that no one in her family—Mom, Gramp, Gram Martha-Jane . . . not even Dad—wanted her to be a quitter. Well, then, she wouldn't be one.

As she hurried from her room, she made herself sing, "I'm a cowgirl . . . yipee-iii-ohhh. I can ride and rope like a cowboy. . . ."

Outside in the backyard, Jess, Cara, and Becky wore cowgirl outfits that matched hers, except for Jess's cut-offs. Jess and Cara rolled out the long, raggedy brown rug on the grass near the patio, while the Funners arrived through the breezeway gate. Becky held the clipboard, writing their names on the check-in list, then sticking name tags on their shirts.

This morning, the Funners seemed more excited than ever, wildly yelling, "Cowboy Day! Cowboy Day!" Mom had sewn red western bandanas for everyone, but most of them already wore bits of western clothes—cowboy hats, shirts, and jeans, and a few clomped along in cowboy boots. They ran straight to the "magic carpet" for the make-believe trip they'd been promised to a western dude ranch.

"Hold everything, buckeroos!" Tricia yelled to them. "I'm glad to see you've remembered Cowboy Day, but let's wait to get on our magic carpet until the rest of the Funners get here. In the meantime, we'll help you put on the red bandanas my mom made for all of us, then you can play on the swings. Your bandanas are on the table. We'll help you put them on."

Mom called out from the kitchen window, "Bryan wants to know if he should play his western songs tape now?"

"Perfect!" Tricia called back. Gram Martha-Jane had found a tape of western songs for Bryan, which he was just barely allowing them to use this morning. "Please tell Cowboy Bryan we really appreciate it. Cowboy Bryan's a-o-kay!"

The Funners crowded around the table for their red bandanas, where Cara and Jess were helping them. Tricia grabbed the schedule and quickly read:

AFTER PARENTS SIGN THE FUNNERS IN:

1. Magic Carpet (Tricia)
2. Western Balloon Fun (Jess)
3. Cowboy Boot Crafts (Becky)
4. Midmorning snacks (Cara)
5. Cowboy Gymnastics (Jess)
6. Finish western crafts. (All help Becky)
7. Free time for swings, etc. (All in charge)

Cowboy music filled the backyard now, starting with "Deep in the Heart of Texas," and the Funners really got excited. Tricia could see why. It looked and sounded as if they were really headed for the Wild West.

Minutes later, the Funners—fifteen of them—were checked in. They'd had more kids on other mornings, but Tricia suspected that this morning fifteen was more than enough.

Time for Cowboy Day to begin, she told herself.

Grabbing a deep breath, she began to twirl her lariat in the air like she'd practiced yesterday after church. Once she had everyone's attention, she let out a loud, "Yippee-i-o-ki-a, b-u-c-k-e-r-o-o-s! Let's get on the m-a-g-i-c carpet for a ride to the Wild West. Yippee-i-o-ki-a!"

The Funners raced for the raggedy rug, and Jess and Cara took their places at the back of it. Becky headed for the middle to help keep the Funners under control.

"Yippee-i-o-ki-a!" everyone sang out with Tricia as they got settled. "Yippee-i-o-ki-a!"

Tricia stood at the front of the rug, whirling her lariat high over her head. "Are you b-u-c-k-a-r-o-o-s ready to ride your horses over the range to a d-u-d-e r-a-n-c-h in Arizona this morning?"

"Yeh! Ready!" the Funners shouted. Someone pounded the rug with excitement, and the rest of them joined in, making puffs of dust rise all over.

"Whoa!" Tricia yelled. "Pull up your red bandanas like real cowboys do. Don't eat that dust!"

"We're *not* eating dust!" Sam Miller objected.

"It's just the way cowboys say it," Tricia explained. "They pull their bandanas up over their noses so they don't inhale so much dust when they're out riding the range. Pull up those bandanas."

The Funners pulled their bandanas over their noses.

"B-u-c-k-e-r-o-o-s!" Tricia called out in her most dramatic voice, "we're headed for a western dude ranch. Now all together, close your eyes and yell, 'Yippee-i-o-ki-a!' "

"YIPPEE-I-O-KI-A!" they shouted at the top of their voices. "YIPPEE-I-O-KI-A!"

Tricia made loud riding noises, "Prrump, prrump, prrump. . . ." and the Funners joined in, bouncing up and down as if they were riding horses.

"Oh, we're r-i-d-i-n-g and r-i-d-i-n-g and r-i-d-i-n-g out on the w-e-s-t-e-r-n r-a-n-g-e!" Tricia called out. "R-i-d-i-n-g and r-i-d-i-n-g and r-i-d-i-n-g along. Prrump, prrump, prrump, prrump. . . ."

They all prrumped again with her, and she heard the tape playing "I'm a Real Cowboy."

"Let's all sing with the tape!" she yelled.

"A cowboy . . . Oh, I'm a cowboy. If you think I can't ride a bucking bronc . . . if you think I can't rope a running steer

. . . then you've never seen a real cowboy . . . yipee-i-o-ki-a."

At the end of the song, she yelled, "Coyotes on the trail! Coyotes! Don't let them spook your horses!"

From the back of the rug, Jess howled like a coyote, "Ar-ar-ouhhh! Ar-ar-ouhhh!"

"Ride 'em cowboys!" Tricia yelled. "Ride right through those coyotes! See, they're scared of us! There! We're leaving them in our dust!"

The Funners looked glad of it, and they prrumped along on their make-believe horses with her.

Suddenly Tricia yelled, "Bad guy! A r-e-a-l bad guy—a horse thief is after us and our horses! R-i-d-e 'em cowboys! R-i-d-e 'em through this canyon . . . quick, around those big rocks and that cactus! R-i-d-e 'em up the hills and through the mountain passes. We can out-ride that horse thief!"

They all prrump-prrump-prrumped wildly, and in case any were peeking, Tricia wound up her lariat and let it fly through the air. "Got 'em!" she yelled, pretending to reel the rope in. "We've got that no-good horse thief. Got 'em . . . and here comes the sheriff to take this no-good guy to jail!"

She put on a deep manly voice, like a sheriff. "Do you b-u-c-k-e-r-o-o-s know there's a big, big reward for catching this here horse thief?"

Tricia spoke in her own voice again. "You don't say, sheriff? How much is the reward?"

The imaginary sheriff said in his low voice, "One m-i-l-l-i-o-n dollars."

She slapped a hand to her mouth with amazement. "Wow, that's a big reward! We can buy lots and lots of horses!"

When they'd finished yelling in agreement, Tricia started "I'm a Real Cowboy," and they all joined in again, bouncing along on their invisible horses and singing out loudly on the "yipee-i-o-ki-a."

Next they tried to sing "Happy Trails to You" with the tape, then "Deep in the Heart of Texas," and finally her all-time favorite, "Cause We'll Always Be Partners."

Finally she and the Funners prrumped back to the ranch.

"Yeah, b-u-c-k-e-r-o-o-s! We made it back to our ranch in Santa Rosita Estates!" she announced into the Funners' wild prrumping. "You can open your eyes now. What a trip! What a trip!"

"Yeh," Bryan said, grinning as he bobbed in place on the rug. "My tape made it good."

"Sure did," Tricia agreed. "You're a top cowboy." She turned to the rest of the Funners. "Next, Jess is going to have a western balloon game for us."

Jess rolled her eyes skyward, probably because she hadn't been able to think of a balloon game that was really western. "Come on, buckeroos!" she called out anyhow. "Hey! We'll make longhorn cattle heads! That's what we'll do. Round balloons for cattle faces and long balloons for their horns."

The Funners scampered off the rug, and Tricia stooped down to roll it up. She watched as the Funners headed for the balloons and began to blow them up. They tried to put them together like cattle heads, but it didn't work. A balloon popped in the sun. "Over in the shade for the cattle balloon game," Jess told them, getting nervous. "What happens when balloons are out in the sun?"

"Popping!" Jojo and Jimjim, the Davis twins, yelled. Excited, their green eyes and the freckles on their faces stood out even more. "Ugga-bugga-bugga-boo!" they added in their secret twin language. "Balloon popping!"

"A balloon fight!" Sam Miller called out. "Let's have a balloon fight!"

"A balloon fight! A balloon fight!" the Funners shouted. They threw themselves right into it, trying to bat one another's balloons, but it was impossible. Next, they began to throw balloons all over the yard. When they tired of that, they sat on and slipped off balloons, popping one after another.

Jojo and Jimjim bellowed another, "Popping! Balloon popping!"

"Yeah, popping!" the others cried out.

Everyone seemed to have decided at once to see who could pop the most balloons the fastest. They jumped on balloons and squeezed balloons. Finally, they stomped on the most stubborn balloons with both feet until they popped, then threw the pieces up in the air like confetti.

In the background, the tape played "Yipee-i-o-ki-a . . . yipee-i-o-ki-a!"

Jess shook her head with hopelessness. "Well, at least the song is western. Who on earth assigned Balloon Fun to me anyhow?"

Becky stood up on a bench by the redwood table. "Now we'll have western crafts," she announced over the yelling kids. "Quiet please, Funners! We'll be drawing our own cowboy boots to take home with us."

Lots of luck! Tricia thought.

At long last, the Funners did settle down around the redwood table and benches. They still prrumped a little along with Bryan's tape of cowboy music, though, and sang out snatches of the songs. And every once in a while, they jumped up to throw bits of balloons into the air before Jess and Cara could pick them all up.

Tricia headed into the house and was glad to see that Mom had made up a tray with tiny paper cups of trail mix and bigger paper cups of orange juice.

"A wild morning!" Mom observed with a laugh.

"Wild, all right," Tricia agreed.

"The Funners will remember Cowboy Day for a long time, maybe all of their lives. Special moments like this are important to everyone. People don't remember days as much as they remember those moments."

"I hope so," Tricia said. "I sure do hope so."

"Of course they will," Mom insisted.

"You think it was that special?"

Her mother nodded, her blue eyes shining. "It was."

Tricia grinned. Special moments or not, she was glad to be inside the quiet house, if only for a few moments. "Guess I'd better turn on Bryan's tape again. Those b-u-c-k-e-r-o-o-s love it."

Heading for the tape player, she realized that she hadn't even thought about Dad and Odette, the missing paintings, or her tryout this afternoon for Alice since the Funners had arrived.

Flipping the cassette over, she remembered.

Dad had given her—and their whole family—lots of special moments. In fact, that's how she knew about horses prrumping . . . and cowboys riding the range . . . and pulling up their bandanas so they wouldn't eat dust. What's more, that's how she knew so much about dude ranches in Arizona. Just last year, he'd taken them to one.

For an instant, she wished she could just keep on being mad-mad-mad at him. Why did she suddenly have to remember his good points? . . . and that people even said she got her wild imagination and flair for the dramatic from him? . . . and that he'd been the one who'd encouraged her to try acting? And, hardest of all, that she still loved him?

CHAPTER

7

Upstairs in her room, Tricia tossed her western hat onto her white wicker desk. She still wore the rest of her cowgirl outfit as she sat down on her bed. Morning Fun for Kids had been great—from Dude Ranch Carpet Ride to Cowboy Boot Crafts and midmorning snacks to Cowboy Gymnastics. And she'd already eaten lunch, finishing it off with the juicy apple she was now munching.

She picked up her *Alice in Wonderland* script, glancing at the places she'd highlighted in yellow for her audition. At least, there was plenty of time before this afternoon's four-thirty audition, even if she didn't feel like practicing. Dad had acted in more plays than she, and he'd always said, "P-r-a-c-t-i-c-e, p-r-a-c-t-i-c-e, p-r-a-c-t-i-c-e!" Back in April, when *Alice in Wonderland* had been announced, he'd also told her, "Kiddo, you'd be a perfect Alice."

A strange idea struck her. *Since Dad did some acting, was*

he only pretending to like Odette? When he was with her, was he acting as if he were someone else?

She chewed down her apple and dumped the core into the wastebasket. No more thinking about them—and no more d-a-w-d-l-i-n-g. Better work on Alice's growing and shrinking, which worked best if she did it like a mime. For growing, she stretched like a sky swimmer for the ceiling; for shrinking, she turned inward on herself like an elf.

Finally satisfied with her growing and shrinking, she faced her make-believe audience. As always, she imagined them to be outside her window, somewhere in the treetops across the street. Taking a deep breath, she began to sing the opening song, "In My World," in her sweetest Alice in Wonderland voice.

Slowly, she danced around the room, pretending to sing to the animals and the flowers. Alice was easy to get into: a dreamer who'd give cats and rabbits little houses and dress them up in shoes and hats and trousers.

After finishing the first few lines of the song, she spun around and faced her audience beyond the window again. Clapping her hands to her mouth in surprise, she exclaimed in her Alice voice, "Why, it's a rabbit wearing a waistcoat . . . and carrying a clock! Oh, Mr. Rabbit, wait! Please wait!"

Rushing to and fro, she pretended to chase him through his rabbit hole, then fall down the deep well below it. "From now on," Tricia-Alice said loudly, for an audience to overhear, "I'll think nothing about simply falling down the stairs at home! Nothing at all!"

She stopped, spun around, and faced her audience again. "I'm growing! I'm growing!" she called out, stretching like a ballerina to giant size. Then, "I'm shrinking!" she cried, shrinking down on herself. Next, she began to bob along in the ocean. "I'm bobbing along in a sea of tears! Dodo Bird, help me! Please help!"

Turning again, she called to White Rabbit, "Oh, your fur and whiskers! You're late . . . you're late . . . you're late!"

After her next turn, she put her hands to her face and pretended to cry. "You foolish Alice," she said tearfully, "you ought to be ashamed of yourself, crying like this."

Next came the Caterpillar, whose question she copied with an equally drawn-out, "W-h-o a-r-e *y-o-u?* Tell me now, w-h-o a-r-e *y-o-u?*"

Last, the cruel Queen of Hearts stood before her.

"Off with my head?!" Tricia-Alice asked in terror. "Off with my head! Oh, please no, your majesty!"

She did the audition again and again. It was short enough to give samplings from the play, but it lasted long enough to show that she could be Alice. Finally, she felt as if she'd been in Wonderland, a strange dreamland. And best of all, her own troubles had disappeared with Alice, down the rabbit hole.

"Enough!" she announced to herself. No sense in more practice, or the fun would whoosh right out of it. Becky would be at home working on a new order of pizza-party invitations, and being with her would help her to forget the audition.

In the hallway, Mom's door was open, and the sewing machine was humming. Tricia stuck her head in. "I'm going to Becky's."

"Are you ready for the audition?" Mom asked. She looked up from the sewing machine, where she was hemming the full skirt of the blue Alice in Wonderland dress.

"As ready as I'll ever be," Tricia answered. "If I practice any more, it'll be dull-dull-dull-dull."

Mom nodded and put on a smile. "Go on. I know you'll be good."

"I wish I did," Tricia said.

As she hurried downstairs, it occurred to her that Mom looked more upset than ever. No, she was probably just imagining that, too!

Minutes later, she pounded out their usual *knock-knock, knock-knock-knock-knock* on Becky's door. She called through the screen, "It's Alice coming back up the rabbit hole."

Oops! Probably Amanda, Becky's five-year-old sister, was napping. Besides, the Hamiltons' house was the smallest model house in Santa Rosita Estates, so you didn't have to yell.

"You wacko!" Becky replied softly as she arrived at the screen door. She was still wearing her cowgirl outfit, too. "I thought you'd be practicing for the audition all afternoon."

"Off with her head!" Tricia replied, raising a mean queen fist to the sky. "Off with her head!"

Rolling her eyes and smiling, Becky let her in. "Sounds like you've practiced too much already."

"Not too much . . . just enough. I figure I've got an hour to donate to making pizza-party invitations before Mom helps me with the makeup. Not that making up for Alice will take much trouble."

"Not with your perfect hair," Becky said. "How are you going to wear it?"

"Pulled back with a headband. White to match my *dainty* apron. Mom is making me an Alice in Wonderland blue dress. We're going to spray my hair even blonder for the audition."

"You'll win the part, that's for sure," Becky predicted. "Anyhow, I'm glad to have you here. It's so quiet when Amanda is napping. Come on."

Tricia followed her to the Hamiltons' small dining area. The table was covered with a sheet of clear plastic, as usual, when Becky did art projects, and the smell of drying salami slices wafted from the nearby kitchen.

"I'm up to drawing the pizzas on the posterboard," Becky explained. "If you really want to help, you can glue on the pepperoni slices and candles."

Tricia settled on the chair across from Becky's and spotted the glue and box of white birthday candles. "Gluing is just my speed. Where are the pepperoni slices?"

"Still in the microwave. I'll get them."

Tricia pulled one of the pale yellow folded posterboard sheets in front of her on the table. Becky had already drawn a pizza on the front, and, inside, she'd carefully lettered:

YOU'RE INVITED
TO A
PIZZA BIRTHDAY PARTY!

DATE:
TIME:
PLACE:

After a moment, Becky put a plateful of pepperoni slices on the table in front of Tricia. "Here, the pepperoni looks dried out enough, but don't get grease on the posterboard."

"You'd think I'd never helped before!"

"Sorry," Becky said, "but I don't have many extra posterboards left."

Tricia nodded, then grinned. "Every time I see these invitations, I think of your famous . . . or maybe I should say *infamous* . . . pizza chase down Ocean Avenue."

Becky gave a laugh and her blue eyes sparkled. "I do, too. It's sure amazing the kind of adventures God gives us if, no matter what happens, we keep thanking Him."

Tricia drew a deep breath, then began to glue dried pepperoni slices on the posterboard pizza. "You know what?"

"What?"

"I forgot all about it . . . that we're supposed to thank Him. I haven't been thanking Him at all."

"Why, Patricia Ellen Bennett! And you're the one who's always telling us—"

"I know it," Tricia said. "It just seems like I'm under a dark cloud lately. I've even been thinking about . . . about dropping out of the Twelve Candles Club."

"Tricia, you can't—"

" . . . and not auditioning for Alice," Tricia continued.

"Tricia!" Becky protested. "If you quit, who could do the Magic Carpet rides? Not one of us! As for you, the next thing, you probably won't want to get up for church . . . and the next thing after that, you'll be quitting everything, and going further and further downhill until you're . . . just plain awful."

"I know it," Tricia admitted, "but I don't want to think about it right now."

"You *have* to think about it, Tricia . . . you have to thank God in everything and trust Him!"

Tricia glued a white birthday candle on a slice of pepperoni. "I just wish you hadn't learned so much about being a Christian! Let's talk about something else."

"Like what?" Becky asked, still upset.

"Like anything else!"

After a long silence, Becky suggested, "You want to practice your audition for Alice? I don't mind hearing it."

"No," Tricia answered. "Before I forget, at the TCC meeting this afternoon, don't tell the others what I just said."

"About quitting?"

Tricia nodded. "Yeah, don't tell them. Anyhow, they know I'll be auditioning today and won't be there."

"Maybe I can get them to help pray for you," Becky said. "I guess you must be nervous."

Instead of replying, Tricia shot Becky an unhappy look. Besides feeling upset about their discussion, she was getting ahead of Becky on the pizza party invitations. "Come on, get working on these and stop talking so much!"

At four o'clock, Mom sat in the driver's seat of the minivan, looking at Tricia as she climbed in beside her. "You're a perfect Alice," she said, her blue eyes full of pleasure. "Perfect . . . blond hair and all."

"Thanks," Tricia replied, then watched her mother's eyes fill with concern again. She'd never say it, Tricia thought, but she was wondering, *Are you nervous?* That—and Dad—must be why she seemed so uptight.

"I'm not nervous," Tricia announced, hoping it would make her mother feel better. She buckled up, then straightened the pages of the play script and her sheet music on her lap. "Anyhow, not real nervous."

Probably Mom was worried about the blond hair spray not washing out—on top of everything else. As they pulled out of the driveway, Tricia told her again, "I know that the hair spray washes out. Kids used it when we did Cinderella, and it always came out."

"Good," Mom said, keeping her eyes on the road.

Tricia glanced out at the neighborhood as they drove along. She wore full makeup, not to mention her new blue Alice dress and white apron. Despite her grumpiness, she knew that her makeup and costume were good, and that her acting was probably better than anyone else's. She also knew *Alice in Wonderland* inside and out—the book and the play and the video. She'd get the part, and life would change for the better. It'd be just like a dream . . . yep, a wonderland . . . and make everyone feel happier.

Luckily, Suzanne and Bryan sat in the middle seat imitating Alice and the white rabbit instead of bothering her with questions. Mom must have known not to ask questions, too, because she talked about how perfect the blue Alice dress was, "Nice and full for graceful curtseys to the mean queen and to the flowers," she said. "The petticoat hangs out from under the dress just enough, too. Wonder if I should have made pantalets for it—"

"It's perfect for now," Tricia assured her. "Perfect."

"Yes, I guess it is," Mom decided. "And your white tights and black ballet shoes are just the right touches."

"Yeh," Tricia agreed, checking her legs and feet. "Almost no one even bothers with costumes for the auditions, but you know—" She stopped herself just in time from saying, *You know how Dad says that bothering with costumes at the audition gives you a winning edge.*

"It was fun to make," Mom said. "And you can always wear the dress—without the petticoat hanging out—as a Sunday dress."

They rode along then in a more comfortable silence, and Tricia thought how good it was to be part of a family. Even with Dad missing, when they rode along in the minivan, it felt as if they were in a warm cocoon together. Hadn't Dad had that feeling of being snug in a family, too?

When they arrived at Santa Rosita Community Church, Mom drove up the drive to the recreation room. "Do you want us to come in?" she asked. "Or should I make a quick stop at Sunshine Nursery? I need to buy some geraniums."

"Buy the flowers," Tricia answered. She opened her door and jumped out. The play auditions were nearly always on time, so she called out, "See you soon!"

Kids were being dropped off or picked up all around, which wasn't surprising, since over two hundred kids were expected to try out. Just a few of them were in some kind of costume, but she didn't see any others dressed as Alice.

Tricia headed behind the minivan and up the steps to the side doors of the room, her script and the sheet music for "In My World" in hand. She must not-not-not forget to give the sheet music to the pianist before she tried out.

Seeing her reflection in the glass door, she told herself, "I'm Alice. I'm Alice in Wonderland."

The recreation room had a yellowish hardwood floor for playing basketball, and the basketball hoops were even down in playing position. The front of the huge room had a big stage with blue velvet curtains pulled aside. Mrs. Plimpton, the pianist, sat at the black baby grand piano just below the stage, and was now playing "Tea for Two."

On the stage, two boys and three girls were auditioning, their arms behind their backs as the dance instructor called out, "One, two, three, turn. Jump! One, two, three, four!"

Watching, Tricia guessed they were trying out for Tweedle-dee and Tweedle-dum, though it could be other parts. They looked scared as anything, like she'd been at her first audition, for *The Wizard of Oz*. And they were trying hard to ignore the row of judges who sat at a line of three long tables in the back of the room. Some of the judges were older kids, and there was the new assistant director, and the director, Kevin Thomas, who'd always praised her acting. Of course, he always called out a "Good!" to everyone else when they finished trying out, too.

Before long, the dance routine was over, and Kevin spoke into his microphone. His voice came out loudly through the loudspeakers. "GOOD. THANK YOU VERY MUCH."

One of the boys took a crazy bow, then rushed off with the others, disappearing beyond the curtains.

"NEXT . . . CHELSEA DOUGLAS, MARILEE CANT-WELL, JOANNA MARSTON, DAVID JENKINS, AND JONATHAN ORTMAN," Kevin's voice boomed through the loudspeakers.

The five kids were already in the wings, and they hurried onto the stage. Tricia glanced at the big clock on the back wall. Four twenty-five. Time to head for the stage herself.

One of the girls onstage said, "I'm Joanna Marston. I'm nine years old, and . . . and I'm trying out for any part."

Her first mistake, Tricia thought. It was smarter to try for a definite part, or say, "I'm trying out for Caterpillar, but I'm open to any other part."

"LET'S HEAR YOU REALLY PROJECT," Kevin boomed. "HOW LOUDLY YOU INTRODUCE YOUR-SELF SHOWS ME HOW WELL YOU CAN PROJECT, AND HOW WILLING YOU MIGHT BE TO MAKE A

FOOL OF YOURSELF. YOU OFTEN HAVE TO BE WILLING TO MAKE A FOOL OF YOURSELF AS AN ACTOR OR ACTRESS."

You know it, Tricia thought. This time when Joanna Marston spoke, she did project.

Tricia headed for Mrs. Plimpton, the pianist, who smiled and nodded as Tricia put her sheet music on the piano.

Once on the side of the stage, she sat down on a folding chair with four other kids. Most looked about twelve, too, except Sandi Steele, who was going into eighth grade. The other girl was dressed all in green, like Peter Pan . . . a strange costume to wear for Alice in Wonderland! Maybe she was just strange, though, because she darted a bewildered glance at Tricia, too.

While the kids onstage auditioned, Tricia watched them and studied the yellow highlighted script parts again. First, most of the kids did songs or speaking parts—or both, like she would. Then came the dance steps, which were usually easy and fun.

When she looked up, one of the boys onstage was singing "Yankee Doodle," swinging his arms hard, and doing a marching routine. Next, one of the girls sang a Christian song, "I'm Giving It Up to You" with a great tape. The last boy sang "This Land Is Your Land" with exaggerated gestures.

Suddenly Kevin's voice boomed "TRICIA BENNETT," along with the names of the four others who waited in the wings with her.

Someone whispered, "Break a leg!" which was stage talk for "good luck."

When they were lined up onstage, Kevin boomed, "TRICIA, WHY DON'T YOU BEGIN?"

Tricia remembered to project her voice. "My name is Tricia Bennett. I'm twelve years old, and I'm auditioning for Alice."

Mrs. Plimpton gave her a strange glance from the piano, then began to play "In My World."

Alice . . . you're Alice, Tricia reminded herself, then began to sing. As the song went on, she knew it sounded just like Alice in Wonderland should. In fact, she felt just like her in her blue dress and dainty white apron. Everyone in the multipurpose room listened with interest.

The moment she finished the first lines, she spun around and faced the audience again. Clapping her hands to her mouth, she exclaimed in her Alice voice, "Why, it's a rabbit wearing a waistcoat . . . and carrying a clock! Oh, Mr. Rabbit, wait! Please wait!"

Rushing to and fro, she pretended to chase him through his rabbit hole, then fell down the deep well below it. "After this," Tricia-Alice announced, "I'll think nothing about simply falling down the stairs at home! Nothing at all!"

In no time at all, she grew and shrunk, bobbed along in the sea of tears, and finished with the Caterpillar and the Queen of Hearts. When she took a bow and stepped back, she knew it was her best-ever audition.

"GOOD!" Kevin's voice boomed through the room. "VERY GOOD, TRICIA, EXCEPT FOR ONE THING. WE'RE NOT DOING *ALICE IN WONDERLAND* NOW. IT WAS CHANGED SOME MONTHS AGO. WE'RE DOING *PETER PAN*."

Tricia stared at him, horrified, then tore off the stage and ran for the side door. No sense in even staying for the dance audition. She'd never in all of her life felt so foolish, so totally embarrassed. Worst of all, everyone in Santa Rosita would know she'd made a fool of herself . . . even if they weren't laughing yet. What they didn't know, though, was that Dad had brought her the script and told her they were doing *Alice in Wonderland*! It was all his fault!

As she raced to the glass doors, she turned for an instant and was glad that at least Kevin was watching the stage, not her. Still rushing, she turned back, and her face smacked against the glass door, leaving a smeared imprint of Alice's makeup. A perfect reminder for everyone of Tricia Bennett's utter disgrace . . . and the fact that she could probably never face them for an audition again!

CHAPTER

8

Minutes later, Mom pulled up in the minivan, and Tricia climbed sadly into the front seat.

"How did the audition go?" Mom asked.

Tricia slammed the van door. "Not one bit good!"

Mom gazed at her for a moment before driving on. "Whatever went wrong?"

"Instead of doing *Alice in Wonderland*, they're doing *Peter Pan*! I feel like the worst fool who's ever lived, and I bet Dad told me wrong on purpose, too."

"I'm sorry to hear it," Mom answered. She drove the van through the church lot toward the street. "I don't think, though, that your father would have purposely misled you."

"I wouldn't be surprised if he did!" Tricia said angrily.

"I would," Mom replied. "Your father has never done anything to purposely hurt you. It's my guess that he didn't know they'd changed plays, either. And you've been so busy this summer with the Twelve Candles Club that I'd guess you didn't even contact the play people."

"I sent in my audition form with my phone number and everything. If they were changing plays, they should have called me!" She didn't even want to think that maybe the change of plays had been mentioned on the audition form. In fact, now that she thought of it, it seemed as if there had been a notice about *Peter Pan*. How could she not have paid attention?

Mom wheeled the van onto the street, then spoke without glancing at Tricia. "I'm sorry to say that I have bad news, too. I didn't want to tell you—or Suzanne or Bryan—until after your audition. I'm afraid that Gramp is very sick. Gram called me at noon. He's had a heart attack."

"What?!" Tricia asked, not believing it.

But Mom looked so serious that it must be true. Suddenly Tricia's own heart hurt.

Suzanne and Bryan quieted behind them, too.

From the backseat, Bryan asked, "Is Gramp going to be dead?"

"Don't say that!" Tricia told him. "Don't say that, Bryan!"

But now Suzanne asked, "Is he though? Is Gramp dying?"

"We hope not," Mom answered, keeping her eye on traffic. "We surely hope not, but his condition is very, very serious."

Suzanne wailed, "I don't want him to die!"

"I don't want him to die, either!" Bryan bawled.

"Don't say that . . . stop it!" Tricia ordered them. But tears from Suzanne's blue-green eyes rolled down her chubby cheeks. And Bryan was beginning to cry, too.

Tricia turned forward, wishing she could cry herself. Instead, her heart hurt and her eyes were as dry as could be.

Everything about her felt numb.

Mom's voice sounded reassuring but sad. "We know that the Lord has prepared a wonderful place for Gramp in heaven. We may not want Gramp to go, but we can't control it."

"We can pray!" Tricia said, determined. "We can pray for him to stay here on earth for a while longer!"

"Yes, we can," Mom agreed. "Believe me, I've been praying exactly that . . . and that at least something good, some kind of a special blessing, would come of all of this."

"What else can we do?" Tricia asked her.

"Not much. I'm going to the hospital tonight. Becky's mother said she'd sit with Suzanne and Bryan. I was sort of hoping you'd go with me for moral support, Trish."

"Me? Me go to the hospital with you?" She'd never been inside a hospital, except to be born.

Mom nodded. "They probably won't let you into intensive care to see him, but I don't feel like going alone."

Probably worried that Dad will be there, Tricia thought.

"You'd cheer up Gram Martha-Jane, too," Mom said. "You know you would."

"I'll go," Tricia decided, even though she didn't want to.

The inside of the van became terribly quiet as they drove on toward Santa Rosita Estates.

Suddenly she remembered. "Oh, no! I'm baby-sitting the Hawkins kids tonight." Probably it would be all right to cancel, but that wasn't the way Twelve Candles wanted to do things. "Maybe Becky can sit for me. I don't think she's busy."

"I hope so," Mom said. After a moment, she added, "I'm sorry about the play, Trish. Maybe you just weren't meant to be in it."

Tricia shrugged. "Probably everyone thought I'd know

about them changing plays. None of that seems so important now. In fact, it hardly seems important at all."

When they arrived at their house, Tricia still felt numb. Instead of running next door to talk to Becky, Tricia headed for the kitchen phone.

Right away, Becky said, "Mom told me your bad news. I was just remembering that your gramp was already sick at the LeRoy party and went home early."

"I forgot that. Anyhow, Mom wants me to go to the hospital with her tonight. Can you sit with the Hawkins kids tonight?"

"Sure," Becky answered. "I thought maybe you'd ask."

"Thanks. It's seven until midnight. Mr. Hawkins picks you up and takes you home."

"I'll call them for you," Becky offered. "I could say there's a problem in your family."

"Please just say 'a sickness in the family,' " Tricia told her. "Everyone in Santa Rosita probably knows about our *other* family problem."

" 'Sickness in the family' is exactly what I'll say," Becky promised. "You know, I've been thinking, you'd better try to look older to get into the hospital or they might not let you in."

The thought hadn't even entered Tricia's mind.

"Wear your green cotton knit dress and a little bit of your hair braided behind your bangs, like you do sometimes. It makes you look older."

"Guess I will."

Becky's friendship helped a lot, Tricia thought, but her spirits drooped again. "With all of this trouble, I really feel like quitting TCC now. Just quitting it and everything else forever and ever!"

"Tricia Bennett, your gramp wouldn't want you to, and you know it! Besides, you wouldn't let me be a quitter when things went wrong in my life. And I told you before, it'd be a poor witness . . . a very, very poor example of your faith to everyone else."

After that, neither of them spoke.

Finally Becky asked, "How'd the play tryout go?"

"Terrible. It was just as terrible as could be. The worst I've ever done. I don't want to talk about it."

"Then we won't," Becky assured her. "But I'm going to be praying for you . . . and for your gramp . . . and your father, too. And I don't care how badly you did at the play tryout. You're still my very best friend."

Hot tears pressed behind Tricia's eyes, and she knew she was going to bawl fiercely. She choked out a "Thanks, Beck," and slammed down the phone.

Tears blinding her eyes, she raced up the stairs to her room. Sobbing, she shut her door and threw herself onto the bed. With Gramp in the hospital, Dad leaving them, and the play disaster, what else could go wrong?

She'd no more than thought it when she knew what would be the worst of all: losing her faith in God.

Please, Lord, she prayed, *help Gramp to get well . . . and make Dad come back to our family.* . . . She remembered that God had promised a special help for those who asked. *And please, Lord, give me more faith!*

I don't want to do this . . . I don't want to do this, she thought as she and Mom drove to the hospital. But, before long, they were parking at Santa Rosita General, which made Gramp's heart attack even more real.

As they walked from the parking lot to the hospital entrance, Tricia hoped they'd let her in. She'd worn her green cotton knit dress, as Becky had suggested, and braided narrow strands of hair above her bangs, too. Besides that, she'd put on a little eye liner and pale lipstick, not enough for Mom to notice in her worried condition. And, in the mirror, she had looked older.

Inside, the hospital entry smelled like cleaning supplies and peroxide. The lady at the desk was friendly, though. She only glanced at Tricia for an instant before saying, "Intensive care is on the first floor. Follow the signs to your right and stop at the nurses' station."

Phew! Tricia thought. She'd gotten in, but the smell was making her dizzy. It was no wonder people in hospitals were sick if they had to breathe this kind of stuff. Just so she didn't see gory operations, like they sometimes showed on the TV news.

"You all right?" Mom asked her. "You look a little white. Maybe I shouldn't have brought you after all—"

"I'll be fine, Mom," Tricia assured her. "I'll be fine."

Mom bit down on her lower lip. "I don't know what I'd do without you, Tricia."

Tricia nodded.

Be strong, Tricia told herself as they walked down the hallway. *Be strong even if I can't stand this smell!*

"You'll probably have to wait in the waiting room," Mom explained. "I may have to, as well. It'll depend on Gramp's doctor's orders, but Gram will be pleased that we've come . . . and Gramp, too."

Finally they arrived at the nurses' station.

"We're Reverend Bennett's family," Mom said.

One of the nurses introduced herself as Lori. "His wife has gone down to the cafeteria to eat. If you'll sit down in the waiting room for a moment, I'll check if you can go in to see him. He's the only patient in intensive care now, and sometimes he's awake."

The waiting room was more cheerful, Tricia noticed as they sat down. But the hospital smell was there, too. She picked up a magazine, but only looked at the pictures.

After a long time, the nurse stuck her head in. "You can both visit Reverend Bennett for five minutes."

Tricia rose to her feet, slightly dizzy, and she felt Mom's arm around her shoulders. "You all right, Tricia?"

"I'm okay," Tricia told her, which wasn't quite true.

They followed the nurse to a nearby door, which she opened. "Only five minutes now."

Inside, Gramp lay in a hospital bed with all kinds of tubes and wires attached to him. For an instant, Tricia thought he was already dead, but then saw he was breathing. At least the white sheet over his body was going up and down.

"Dad?" Mom whispered to him, even though she was really his daughter-in-law. "Dad . . . it's Susie and Tricia. We've come to see you."

He opened his nice gray-blue eyes and smiled at them. "Thanks for coming. . . ."

"We're praying," Mom said. "We're all praying for you."

He nodded, still smiling. "Jesus is, too."

Tricia knew what he meant . . . that Jesus was on the right hand of God, praying for all of His people, which was a little hard to understand since He was in their hearts, too.

"We love you," Tricia told him.

Gramp's eyes shone. "I love you, too. Don't ever forget that. I love you."

It almost sounds as if he's saying goodbye! Tricia thought in alarm. Tears burst to her eyes. "Gramp, get well. Please, get well!"

He only nodded. "We'll see what the Lord has in mind."

"We need you," she whispered, trying to blink the wetness in her eyes away. "We really need you here."

"You need your father more," he whispered. "Pray for him like never before."

"We are," Mom told him, tears running down her face now, too. "We'd better let you rest now. We'll be out in the waiting room."

He smiled, then seemed to drift off to sleep again.

Out in the hallway, Tricia felt dizzy again. From the corner of her eye, she saw two familiar figures approaching.

Dad and Odette LeRoy!

She couldn't believe it! He'd actually bring Odette to the hospital with him!

Mom stared at them in amazement, too.

"I didn't expect to see you two here," Dad said, looking a little embarrassed.

Mom seemed hurt, softening her voice. "I didn't expect to see you two, either."

"I'm taking a week off work and staying with my mother so she's not alone," Dad explained.

Odette twisted her car keys, as usual, and began to pick at a smudge of grease under one of her long fingernails. "And I'm visiting my grandparents here in Santa Rosita."

But, seeing them here together, Tricia felt more hurt than she'd ever been in her life. But, more than that, she felt anger.

She clenched her fists and stared at Odette. "You've got nerve, coming here to the hospital!"

"Tricia!" Mom scolded, looking shocked and embarrassed.

Odette reached for Dad's arm, grasping hold of it. "Your father asked me to come with him. After all, Reverend Bennett *is* his father."

Tricia turned her angry stare on him. She felt like saying *You should have known Mom would be here. She loves your father—your own father—more than you do!* But something inside stopped her.

As she struggled to contain her anger, the hallway and its smell began to spin around her. Her stomach looped over as everything turned gray, then grayer and grayer. Suddenly, she saw the floor coming up to meet her, and everything disappeared as she fainted away.

CHAPTER

9

The next morning, Becky phoned. "Bad news," she said. "You'll never guess what happened."

Tricia shook her head, still not quite awake. "What?"

"It's about the missing paintings. The LeRoys' insurance investigator and a police detective are snooping around about us now! They seem to think that we . . . I mean the TCC . . . are the main suspects!"

"The main suspects?! You're kidding."

"I'm not," Becky answered. "What should we do?"

Tricia's head began to spin again. "I don't know," she said into the phone. "I still don't feel right. I fainted last night at the hospital."

"You did what?" Becky demanded.

"Fainted!" Tricia could scarcely believe it herself. "Everything started spinning, and I fainted right there in the hospital."

"Why?"

"It sure wasn't on purpose!" Tricia assured her. "I think it was partly seeing Gramp in the hospital bed and partly the hospital smell."

"What happened then?"

"When I woke up, there were nurses all around me, and I had to ride in a wheelchair to get examined by a doctor."

"I can't believe it!" Becky said.

"I couldn't, either," Tricia answered. "The only good thing about it was that Odette started feeling queasy and went outside to her car. Finally Dad went with Mom to see Gramp. Just the two of them."

Tricia wasn't about to tell Becky, but Mom said Gramp had told them he was glad to see them back together again . . . that God had put them together in marriage, and that He didn't intend for them not to stay that way. Neither of them had wanted to upset Gramp with the truth.

"And your gramp's okay?"

Tricia nodded as if Becky were right there instead of on the phone. "He's a little bit better. They're going to try him on some medicine today, so please keep praying."

"Did your gram see Odious Odette there?"

"Nope. Odette was gone by the time Gram Martha-Jane arrived. And you know Gram Martha-Jane. After she saw I was okay, she almost laughed because she fainted once in a hospital in Georgia when she was my age. I guess it's not all that strange for visitors to faint."

"Leave it to you to do something dramatic," Becky said. "You didn't hurt your head or anything?"

"My head is too hard for hurting. But the doctor said I should rest today, and that means no Morning Fun for Kids.

You can still use our backyard, and Mom says she'll stay nearby to help."

Becky groaned. "It'll be dreadful without you to do the Magic Carpet ride, especially after Cowboy Day. The Funners will be expecting something even better!"

"I'm sorry. Actually, I do feel tired."

Becky's voice filled with panic. "Are you going to faint again?"

"I don't think so, but I'm going back to bed. How did sitting for the Hawkins kids go?"

"Terrible!" Becky answered. "Two of them threw up. Mom figures it's the one-day stomach flu that's going around."

"Yipes!"

"Just see if I take one of your baby-sitting jobs again!"

Tricia knew by her friend's tone of voice that she was only teasing. "I'm going back to bed. I'm afraid I'll miss another TCC meeting this afternoon. You can tell them what happened."

Later, when Tricia heard car doors slamming and the Funners' voices, she was too tired to even go to the window to watch them. When Morning Fun for Kids ended, Mom reported that the morning had gone well, but the Funners had missed their Magic Carpet ride. Also that Gramp was a little bit better.

Tricia felt badly about missing the TCC activities, but she had a feeling that she'd better be rested for whatever might lie ahead. As it was, they had to decide what to do about the police and insurance investigator.

The next morning, Becky phoned her again. "I'm the one who's sick now. Mom thinks I got the stomach flu from the

Hawkins kids. I've been throwing up."

"Urk . . . I'm sorry!"

"You'll be sorrier when you hear my other problem," Becky said. "I've already called Jess and Cara, and they're both busy. This is the morning I'm supposed to baby-sit Jojo and Jimjim Davis from ten to twelve. And from one to three this afternoon, dog-sit Yvette. I was hoping you'd take the jobs since there's nobody else—"

"Me, dog-sit Yvette?!" Tricia yelled into the phone. "I'll sit with Jojo and Jimjim, but no way will I dog-sit Yvette! No way!"

"There's no one else to do it, Tricia," Becky said, pleading. "It's Mrs. LeRoy who called, because she has to go to a meeting. I don't want to let her down. She was so nice and generous when we worked at their party. Anyhow, it's only for two hours and Odette won't even be home."

Tricia felt suspicious. "How do you know?"

"Because Mrs. LeRoy told me she's going down to Mexico for the day."

"Probably with my dad since he's taken the week off."

"I don't know," Becky answered. "Anyhow, can you please dog-sit for me, too? Besides, maybe you can snoop around to find out more about the missing paintings while you're there. That's what I was going to do."

"You think they might still be there, Beck?"

"Who knows? Maybe. It would sure be great if we could find out something before we have to talk to that police detective. It feels horrible not to know *anything*."

Tricia still didn't feel quite right about going to the LeRoys' estate. "You sure about Odette not being there?"

"That's what Mrs. LeRoy told me."

"Okay then, I'll do it," Tricia finally decided. "But only because you're my best friend. As for the missing paintings— what about the police and the insurance investigator?"

"The insurance investigator wants to have a meeting with us tomorrow so he can ask us questions."

"Tomorrow?!" Tricia repeated.

"Yeah. To-mor-row."

"Umpty-dumpty-um-dum-a-lum!" Jojo and Jimjim hollered when Tricia walked into their house.

Despite all of her troubles, Tricia had to laugh. She knew it was the four-year-old boys' secret twin language. "Same to you!"

Their mother, Mrs. Davis, had been her second-grade teacher, and she laughed, too. "Good thinking, Tricia Bennett. Don't let them bamboozle you."

"Bamboozle?"

Mrs. Davis laughed again. "Don't let them trick you. They're getting into more and more mischief nowadays."

Tricia let out a worried "Oh-oh!"

"Remembering you from school, I'd say they're not apt to get ahead of you, if you watch them," Mrs. Davis assured her. "They'd probably like to play outside. If they seem tired, they adore their *Babar the Elephant* video. And, if they're hungry, there's peanut butter, jelly, and bread. Milk in the fridge. I'm off to a library meeting."

Not surprisingly, Mrs. Davis was well organized. She'd already filled out the TCC baby-sitting form with the phone number of the library, emergency information like the doctor's name and number, and everything else, and stuck it up by the kitchen phone.

"Have fun!" she called out to them. "I'll be back soon."

"Urga-burga-boom!" the twins yelled at their mother.

It sounded almost like a threat, but the boys were so good-natured, they were soon smiling. "Outside!" they yelled to Tricia. "Let's go outside!"

"Good idea," Tricia agreed. She opened the back door and let them into their fenced backyard. They had cute freckled faces and dark curly hair, and their mischievous green eyes were like her own. She looked out at their yard. "Whoa! You've got a nice swing set. You want me to push you?"

"Yeah! Push . . . push . . . push!" they answered.

It was going to be a good morning, Tricia decided. "Hey, you guys, you're special," she told them. "I really like you. And don't you look nice in those green shorts and checkered tops with your green eyes. I'd like some to match."

They grinned happily and gave her another "Umpty-dumpty-um-dum-a-lum!"

It sounded a lot like "We like you, too."

They squealed with delight as she pushed them on their swings, then were as happy as could be as she "drove" their trucks around in the sandbox, often giving out a loud "Honk! Honk!" with them.

"Cowboy story . . . cowboy riding," they asked.

She found a long lounge cushion, and they settled down on it, pretending to be riding the range, prrumping along on invisible horses again.

Just before noon, Tricia decided to clean them up and make lunch. Peanut butter and jelly sandwiches weren't much trouble, but Mrs. Davis would probably be glad to see that they'd already been fed.

At noon, the kitchen phone rang.

Tricia picked up the receiver. "Davis residence."

It was Mrs. Davis, sounding upset. "I'm sorry to report that I'm having a problem. My car broke down on the freeway, and I've had to call a tow truck. Can you sit with the boys this afternoon?"

"I . . . I'm sorry, but I have to dog-sit for Mrs. LeRoy from one to three."

"Oh, dear," Mrs. Davis replied, then her voice turned thoughtful. "Well, I do know Mrs. LeRoy, and she's quite nice. Perhaps the best plan is for me to call her. I'll ask if she'll pick you and the boys up at my house, then take you to her house until I can get there. I'll call you right back."

Moments later, Mrs. Davis phoned again. "Bless her heart, Mrs. LeRoy didn't mind at all. She'll pick you all up around twelve-thirty, and I'll come by for the boys at the LeRoy house as soon as I can."

"Okay," Tricia said. It was getting complicated, but it sounded as if it would be all right . . . unless Mrs. LeRoy suspected them of stealing the paintings, too! Better let Mom know about the change of plans, Tricia decided, and phoned.

At twelve-thirty, Mrs. LeRoy drove up in her tan Cadillac, smiling and not seeming at all distrustful. Yvette sat beside her on the passenger seat. She didn't look distrustful, either, only like a very haughty black poodle. The moment she saw the boys, though, she took an interest.

"Well, isn't this going to be fun for Yvette!" Mrs. LeRoy remarked. "Despite her superior manner, she does love children. Sometimes you'd think she were one of them."

Tricia drew a deep breath. "I'm glad to hear it. I guess we'll sit in back."

The twins climbed in with Tricia, and she sat in the middle

and helped them buckle up. "Urga-burga-burga-boo!" they said, pointing at Yvette.

Mrs. LeRoy laughed, and Yvette looked back at them excitedly and gave a loud "Woof!"

"They speak in a secret twin language sometimes," Tricia explained to Mrs. LeRoy.

"Isn't that fun?" was her reply. "Sometimes I wish I had a secret language of my own."

The twins grinned. "Urga-burga-burga-boo!" they said, pointing now at Mrs. LeRoy.

Mrs. LeRoy laughed heartily.

It was hard to believe that Odette was her granddaughter, Tricia thought again.

When they arrived at her estate, Mrs. LeRoy said, "It would be better if you stayed outside with the boys since our house isn't very child-proof."

And her paintings and other valuables are inside the house, too, Tricia thought. *Fat chance to snoop around for the missing paintings outside.*

A second later, however, something different occurred to her. Maybe Mrs. LeRoy didn't suspect them. After all, she'd called Becky—a member of the TCC—to dog-sit. Surely she wouldn't ask any of them if she were suspicious.

Mrs. LeRoy was saying, "We do have an old playhouse out in the backyard for when children visit. It's shaded by a big pepper tree, so it's cool. I think Jojo and Jimjim might enjoy it."

When they drove around back and saw the big playhouse, Jojo and Jimjim let out a wild "Urga-burga-boo-playhouse!"

Yvette jumped out of the car after them, woofing and waving her tail wildly.

Mrs. LeRoy smiled at them. "If anyone needs a drink of water or has to go to the bathroom, my housekeeper, Marta, is in the house to let you in."

"Thanks," Tricia told her. She remembered Marta from the party.

"Have fun," Mrs. LeRoy told them and drove off.

As Tricia chased the twins and Yvette to the playhouse, she noticed Odette's white Corvette was parked in the garage. Probably they had driven Dad's older car down to Mexico, though a white Corvette was bound to impress him.

If only she could somehow show him that Odette was no good, despite her expensive things! Well, there was no use in worrying about them.

"It looks like a nice playhouse," she said to the twins. "Let's see what's in it." *Maybe the missing paintings?*

Instead, there was a lot of kid-size red and blue furniture. But the two-room playhouse was so big that there was even an old desk and a beat-up office chair on wheels. "Go-go!" Jojo and Jimjim yelled, sitting on the office chair and beginning to roll around the room. Hangers in the little closet held old red and blue sweatshirts, and cute pictures for kids hung on the walls, but there was no sign of the stolen paintings.

Jojo and Jimjim made themselves at home, as did Yvette. They even pretended the big black poodle was a lion who'd come to live with them in the playhouse, and Yvette enjoyed all of the attention. Next, Yvette became a horse, and they turned into cowboys. Between their *Urga-burga-boo-cowboy!* yells, Tricia was enjoying them a lot. They sure had crazy imaginations—like hers.

After a long time, Jojo announced, "Want a drink!"

"Want a drink!" Jimjim echoed.

They sang out together, "Want a drink . . . want a drink . . . drink, drink, drink, drink!"

Tricia didn't blame them. The playhouse was shaded, but it was still a hot afternoon. "Okay, okay. If you promise to stay here and be good, I'll go in and ask for some glasses and a pitcher of water. But you have to promise to be good."

"We be good," Jojo answered.

Jimjim repeated, "We be good."

"Let's hope so," Tricia said and headed for the house. One thing she'd never considered was that Marta, or other household help, might have stolen the missing paintings. She'd been so busy at the party, that she hadn't really paid much attention to them. Of course, they had been busy, too.

As she arrived at the back door, Marta was already holding it open for her. Probably watching them through the kitchen window. *"Buenas tardes,"* Marta said, smiling.

Tricia remembered her from the Fourth of July party, and remembered some Spanish she had learned from Cara. *"Buenas tardes, Señora."*

Marta's brown eyes sparkled. "Nice to see you again. Please come in."

"We're all thirsty," Tricia told her. "Mrs. LeRoy said to ask for water. Do you have a plastic pitcher and glasses so the boys don't break them?"

"Sí," Marta answered. "Even a plastic tray."

Marta seemed very friendly, Tricia thought as she followed her into the kitchen. She decided to take a chance. "We're awfully worried about the stolen paintings. Have you heard anything about them?"

Marta's brown eyes flashed with interest, then she opened a kitchen cabinet. *"Nada* . . . nothing. I don't take them."

"I didn't think you would," Tricia said. "But the police think that *we* did! Do you know anything that might help us?"

Marta's eyes darted out the kitchen window toward the carport, then she gave Tricia a long and meaningful look. An instant later she shook her head. "*Nada* . . . I know nothing. Let me get you cold water from the refrigerator."

As Marta turned away, Tricia glanced out the window. Beyond the garage was a three-car carport, where only Odette's white Corvette stood. Was Marta trying to give her a hint? Probably Odette was nasty to household help, too. If only there were a way to check out Odette's car!

Suddenly Tricia recalled the grease under Odette's fingernails at the hospital. Surely she hadn't worked on the Corvette's motor or changed its tires herself. There must be another reason. . . .

When Tricia stepped out the back door with a tray holding the pitcher and glasses, she almost screamed in terror. Out on the driveway, Jojo and Jimjim had tied the sleeve of a red sweatshirt to Yvette's rhinestone collar, and the boys gripped the other end of the sweatshirt, stretching it way out. Sitting in the old office chair, they were rolling down the driveway on its wheels, while the poodle pulled them as fast as he could by the red sweatshirt.

"Giddi-up!" Jojo and Jimjim yelled at Yvette. "Giddi-up!"

"Stop that, you crazy kids!" Tricia shouted. "Stop that right now! You're going to fall off that chair and get all skinned up!"

She plopped the tray down and raced after them. "Stop, Yvette! S-t-o-p!!!"

But Yvette ran on, and the twins yelled louder than ever. "Giddi-up, Yvette! Giddi-up!"

Tricia raced along the driveway to catch them.

Yvette and the office chair holding Jojo and Jimjim sped up down the hill. Worse, a big hole in the driveway lay ahead.

"Don't hit that hole!" Tricia hollered, running after them. "Don't hit it! Head for the lawn!"

Scared, the twins bawled, "Help us! Help us!"

Just before the chair wheels hit the rut, Tricia threw her arms around the boys and the chair back. "Let go of that sweatshirt! Let go this minute!"

They looked scared, but they let loose, and she held on to them and the chair, pumping her legs toward the lawn. As soon as they hit it, all three of them tumbled onto the grass.

Behind them on the driveway, Yvette slowed, the red sweatshirt trailing behind her.

"Whew! You k-i-d-s!" Tricia howled.

Getting up, she saw Jojo and Jimjim rising to their feet, too, both of them grinning hard. "I told you to stay in the playhouse!"

The boys stole guilty glances at each other.

She put on a gruff voice. "Go get that red sweatshirt. Yvette's left it on the driveway."

She watched them run for it, then hug "good old Vette," as they called her. At least there wasn't blood all over them and they weren't bawling. No damage done.

Jojo and Jimjim brought the red sweatshirt and Yvette back up the driveway with them. "Urga-burga-boo! Urga-burga-boo!" the twins yelled. It sounded as if they were saying *F-U-N . . . F-U-N . . . F-U-N!*

"Come on," she told them. "Just see if I ever baby-sit for you wild kids again!"

They just grinned.

As they made their way past the carport, Tricia glanced at Odette's white Corvette. Now was her chance to check it for the paintings. Now!

She glanced up toward the kitchen. *Ufffff!* Marta was watching from the window. As if that weren't enough, two cars roared up the driveway.

Yipes . . . in them were Mrs. LeRoy and Mrs. Davis! She'd have to find another way to check Odette's car for the missing paintings. And it was important to check the white Corvette before Odette left for Los Angeles.

Maybe later, at this afternoon's meeting, they'd dream up something to save them from suspicion—and save the Twelve Candles Club's reputation.

Only she didn't know what.

CHAPTER

10

Tricia picked up Becky next door, then they headed along the sidewalk toward Jess's house for the TCC meeting. "You sure you feel all right, Becky?" Tricia asked. She slipped her treasurer's report notebook under her arm.

"I'm fine. I felt all right by noon." Becky tucked her long dark hair back under her white headband. "What I wouldn't have given to have seen Yvette pulling Jojo and Jimjim down the LeRoys' driveway!"

"It was wacko, all right." She peered up at a tree just over them. "And I've got an even more wacko suspicion about the stolen paintings—"

"W-h-a-t?" Becky asked, stopping in her tracks. "What about the paintings?!"

"Come on, we'll be late. I'll tell it to everyone just once at Jess's."

"Well, okay, but I am *not* going to be patient!"

Jess's two-story stucco house was just ahead—a big house, and the only custom house in all of Santa Rosita Estates. Its size was a good thing, because it gave them privacy and plenty of room for their meetings. Several years ago, the McColls had remodeled their three-car garage into a room for Jess. It resembled a gym as much as it did a bedroom, full of her gymnastics equipment and posters.

"You missed the last two meetings," Becky reminded Tricia.

"I know it. First, there was the play audition, also known as Disaster Number One. Then yesterday, I still felt wobbly from having fainted at the hospital, which was Disaster Number Two. I prayed that trying to get the paintings won't turn out to be Disaster Number Three."

"Trying to get back the paintings? You mean, you know where they are?"

"Never mind!" Tricia answered.

She saw Cara coming from her front door across the street from Jess's house. "Hey, Cara!"

"Tricia, you're back!" Cara called. "I thought maybe you were dropping out of the club."

"Not me!" Tricia shot a suspicious glance at Becky.

"I didn't say a word!" Becky insisted.

Tricia turned to Cara as she joined them. "Monday was the audition, a disaster I'd rather not discuss . . . and Tuesday, I didn't feel well, which I'd rather not discuss, either."

"Well, I'm glad you're back," Cara said. "What's doing?"

"I think I know about the stolen paintings, but I'll tell it to everyone at once."

Cara breathed a surprised "Whoa!"

Grinning, Tricia headed for Jess's door, but before she

could give their usual *knock-knock, knock-knock-knock-knock*, Jess opened it. Her hazel eyes sparkled. "Well if it isn't the four klutzes back together again!"

They all laughed.

"Tricia has something on the stolen paintings," Cara said.

Jess's mouth opened wide. "You're kidding!"

"Let's sit down first," Tricia suggested. She tried to sound calm, but it was hard to contain her excitement. "We're all in this as a club, and I think we ought to discuss taking . . . ah . . . dangerous chances in a businesslike way."

"Taking dangerous chances!" Jess repeated.

Becky rolled her eyes. "You mean I'm supposed to conduct the meeting . . . and we're supposed to take phone calls and all . . . while you tell?"

Tricia nodded. "That way no one can say I rushed them into doing something dangerous. We'll each have to think hard about it. Maybe we could take the phone off the hook, though."

Becky jerked the phone off the hook, then sat backwards on Jess's desk chair. "In that case, this meeting of the Twelve Candles Club shall now come to order. Will Secretary Cara Hernandez please read the minutes of the last meeting?"

Cara drew a breath, then began to read off the jobs that had been offered and accepted at the last meeting.

"Will Tricia Bennett please read the treasurer's report?" Becky asked with impatience.

As she read, Tricia felt their tension . . . tension that did not concern how much money was in the treasury. When she finished, no one even discussed her treasurer's report.

"Any old business?" Becky asked.

Tricia raised her hand. "I have some old business about the

LeRoy party job and the stolen paintings."

"Get on with it!" Becky said. "What about them?"

Tricia hesitated, then plunged in. "I think maybe the paintings are in Odette's Corvette."

"You're kidding!" Jess answered. "How come?"

"Well, I had to work for Becky today because she was sick . . . baby-sit Jojo and Jimjim this morning, then dog-sit Yvette this afternoon. What happened was Mrs. Davis had car trouble, so I had to take the twins over to the LeRoy house."

They were beginning to look impatient, so she said, "Now here's what's important. When I went to the kitchen for water for the kids, I asked the housekeeper, Marta, if she knew anything about the stolen paintings. She said *nada*, but her eyes shot straight to Odette's white Corvette in the carport and stayed on it for a good long time. She doesn't want to get in trouble, and if anyone ever asks us, we'll just have to say we had a secret message. A s-e-c-r-e-t message."

They were all quiet for a moment. Finally Jess asked, "That's the only clue?"

Tricia nodded. "That's it."

"What could we do?" Cara asked.

"I thought about telling the police," Tricia said, "but they'll ask why Odette would steal the paintings from her own grandparents' house . . . and a thousand other things to make us look ridiculous. Same deal if we tell our parents, and I've got the double problem of Dad dating Odette. It'll just look like I'm trying to make trouble for them. So I figure, the only thing we can do is find the paintings in her car, and make sure Odette gets blamed for it . . . that is, *if* she took them."

"But why *would* she steal her grandparents' paintings?" Becky asked.

Tricia shook her head. "The only reason I can think of is that she doesn't have enough money to keep up her expensive tastes. Besides, she goes gambling a lot in Las Vegas." She thought for a moment, then said, "I've been thinking too, that working for an art gallery would help her know how to sell them off quickly."

"If she did take them, you know she wouldn't put them in the trunk or under the car seats," Jess said. "Where else could we look?"

"Well, I've been doing a little investigating of my own," Tricia said, grinning mischievously. She drew in a deep breath. "I called the Corvette dealer, using my grown-up voice, of course. I said I was working on a mystery story—which *is* kinda true—and asked where a good place would be to hide small paintings in a Corvette."

"You didn't!" Cara said with disbelief.

Tricia nodded. "I did. Anyhow the salesman was glad to help. He said that if he wanted to hide something, he'd take out the spare tire and put the paintings in there. The funny thing is, I saw some spare tires in the LeRoys' carport."

"Spare tires for a Corvette?" Jess asked.

"I don't know," Tricia admitted. "That was before I called the car salesman, so I didn't think much about it."

"What if the car has a security alarm?" Cara asked.

"We'll just have to chance it," Tricia answered. "I figure if the car is parked behind that big locked security gate, maybe Odette wouldn't bother with the security alarm. Besides, she's sort of careless."

Jess raised her brows. "I hope so. So what'll we do?"

"Before sunset, I think we should ride our bikes out to the LeRoy estate. If the big gate is closed, we get our bikes over

119

the nearby fence. If the gate's open, we lift our bikes over the driveway security cord that rings the bell in the house, then sneak up to the garage and hunt for the paintings."

"What if someone sees us?" Cara asked. "They'll think we're trying to steal the car, too!"

"That's why we need darkness. I checked the newspaper for the time of sunset. It's eight twenty-three. What we do is give ourselves ten minutes of darkness to find the paintings, so we start looking with flashlights at eight thirty-three. Before we leave home, we set every alarm clock in our houses for eight forty-three, and leave notes under them. We write something like *We're at the LeRoys' carport. We believe the missing paintings are hidden in Odette LeRoy's white Corvette and that she stole them. Please call the police and tell them N-O-W.*

"What if we're wrong?" Becky asked, her blue eyes wide.

Tricia shrugged. "Then they'll probably arrest us for 'breaking and entering' or something like that. Or they'll give us a stern lecture. Besides, it'd be better to have the paintings found than for them to be suspicious of us forever! And it'd show Dad what Odette's really like."

"I guess so," Jess said. "And you know what? It sounds like fun . . . like a real adventure! I say we go for it!"

"Yeah, let's," Becky agreed. "It's our best chance."

"I guess so," Cara put in.

"Okay," Tricia said. "Here's the plan, if everyone agrees. We meet at my house at seven forty-five, ride our bikes to the LeRoy estate, hope like anything that Dad and Odette aren't back from Mexico yet, then find the paintings just before the police come."

"What if something goes wrong?" Cara asked.

"Then we'll be exactly where we are now . . . under suspicion," Jess said.

"Anyone have a better plan?" Tricia asked.

No one did.

They replaced the phone on the receiver and began to answer calls for the Twelve Candles Club. At five-thirty, they all headed out.

"Remember, seven forty-five in front of my house," Tricia reminded them. "Wear dark jeans and tops. And don't forget to set the alarm clocks all over your houses for eight forty-three and have the notes under them. And don't tell anyone else!"

At seven forty-five, Tricia rode her bike out of her garage. She wore a book bag on her back with a set of wrenches in it. "Ready?" she asked as Jess, Cara, and Becky rode up.

"Ready," they answered. "Anything new?"

"Yep—some good news! Gramp's out of the hospital. He just has to take medicine. The doctors think he'll be fine."

"All right!" her friends called out.

"God sure did answer my prayers," Tricia told them, then called out a "Thank you, Lord!"

They rode off down La Crescenta and headed east in the bike lane on Ocean Avenue. Usually Jess led the way, since she was the strongest and most athletic, but this time, she didn't, and Tricia knew she was in charge.

Okay, God, she prayed, *this is it! With Dad gone, I feel like it's what I'm supposed to do. Please keep us safe.*

She'd been tempted to tell her mother, but she and Gram had been busy getting Gramp from the hospital and fussing over him. No sense upsetting them about this. Besides, none of her friends were supposed to tell.

Ocean Avenue became steeper and steeper as they pedaled uphill. It still wasn't very dark, but Tricia could see the reflectors on her friends' bikes glinting off the streetlights. The scary words rolled through her head again: *The jungle is a dark, dank place . . . of thumping drums and slithering snakes . . . of nighttime screams and daytime shakes. . . .*

Tricia shook off the scary thoughts, determined not to let fear control her. Feeling better, she rode on.

They began to wind up the hillside into the orange groves, where houses stood on acres and acres of land. She craned her neck to look up to where the LeRoy house should be and saw it high in the distance. Glancing back, she was glad to see her three friends pedaling along behind her in the growing darkness.

When they arrived at the LeRoy estate, the huge white moat door still stood open. Relieved, they rode their bikes up the driveway to the security cord, and climbed off their bikes, lifting them over. When they were all on the other side of the cord, they stashed their bikes in the orange grove at the side of the driveway.

When the four of them reached the back of the house, the sky was perfectly dark, except for a light above the kitchen door. In its glow, they could see that Odette's car was still the only one in the carport.

The four of them tiptoed up to the fancy sports car.

"How'll we get the car keys?" Jess whispered.

"Don't need 'em," Tricia whispered back. "The spare tire is kept under the car." She took off her book bag and unzipped it. "I brought some different-sized wrenches."

"Good thinking," Becky whispered.

Crickets chirped in the dark carport and, in the distance,

coyotes yowled. From deep in the house, Yvette gave a woof, then quieted. The sound of a TV show came from somewhere inside, too. Probably Mr. and Mrs. LeRoy were home watching TV, since Yvette couldn't bear to be left alone.

Getting down on her knees on the concrete, Tricia spotted the spare tire space. And there was the metal nut and bolt for opening it!

Scooting into position, a new thought hit: Here's how Odette would get grease on her hands. Surer than ever, Tricia set to work with the wrench, wishing she weren't so clumsy.

Suddenly blue and red lights flashed across the garage as a police car roared up the driveway.

"It's way too early for them!" Tricia hissed.

Yard lights went on, and a policeman leaped from his car. "Freeze! Police! Stand up with your hands in the air!"

The wrench clattered to the ground as Tricia jumped to her feet, her hands high. Her friends' hands were up, too.

"Well, well," the policeman said, "if it isn't you girls again."

Tricia recognized Officer Drane, the same tall policeman who'd questioned them about the burglar at Jess's house last month. Only then they'd all been wearing clown suits.

The officer shook his head and took his hand off his holstered gun.

His partner, Officer Salvio, got out of the driver's seat and asked, "What are you girls up to this time?"

Tricia drew a deep breath. "Someone gave us a secret message that the LeRoys' stolen paintings were hidden in Odette LeRoy's car. We were going to look in the spare tire place."

"I see," Officer Drane replied. "Well, I'm glad you left

notes at your houses. It makes everything a little more believable."

One of our mothers must have found the notes early, Tricia decided, almost thankful for the mess-up.

"Okay, let me have a look down there." He took her wrench and, getting halfway under the car, set to work.

After a minute, he said, "You're right about one thing. That's no spare tire under here . . . not surrounded by a pillowcase and cotton batting."

He got to his feet and peered into the pillowcase. "Looks to me like the missing paintings, all right. We'll take them down to the station for fingerprints—"

Just then Dad's car roared up the driveway, and Odette jumped out. Her red silk dress shimmered under the lights as she shouted, "What are you doing with my car?"

"Looking for stolen paintings," the policeman replied.

"Do you have a search warrant?" she demanded.

Tricia's father stared at Odette. "Hey, the police are on our side. What do you mean *do they have a search warrant*?"

"Just what I said," she retorted angrily.

"As a matter of fact, we do have a search warrant," Officer Drane answered. "We called a judge for it right off."

Mr. LeRoy stepped out the door, followed by his wife. "What's going on out here?"

Officer Drane held up the white pillowcased package. "It appears these girls found your missing paintings hidden in your granddaughter's car." He folded back the pillowcase and held away the cotton batting. "If you'd please look at them for identification—"

Both Mr. and Mrs. LeRoy shot discouraged glances at Odette, then stepped forward to look at the paintings.

"Yes," Mr. LeRoy said. "Those are the missing paintings." He looked at his granddaughter. "What do you have to say for yourself, this time?"

She clenched her fists. "I needed money for bills and you refused to give me more!"

Mr. LeRoy asked, "Gambling bills, Odette?"

She nodded, furious. "What of it?"

Tricia saw her father look at Odette in amazement, then back away in shock. "You never told me—"

"Tell you what?" she snapped at him. "You with your thin wallet! You'd already given me everything I'd ever get out of you! You and that goody-goody minister father . . . and your wife and kids! I was sick to death of hearing about them. As it was, tonight was goodbye!"

Dad clenched his own fists in anger. "I can't believe you'd be so callous—"

Mr. LeRoy interrupted Dad with regret. "If it's any comfort to you, you're not the first man she's fooled. Actually, you're lucky to get out now."

"Well!" Odette huffed.

Officer Drane asked the LeRoys, "Do you wish to press charges for the theft of the paintings?"

"Yes," Mrs. LeRoy said firmly. "For a change, Odette's going to pay for her actions. It's not the first time she's tried to take advantage of us."

Suddenly Odette was being handcuffed, read her rights, and taken away to the police car. Under the outdoor lights, it was an eerie sight . . . the police car driving away into the darkness, and the rest of them standing unhappily on the driveway.

Tricia's heart went out to her father, and she put her arms

around him. "I love you," she whispered. "I really love you, Dad . . . and not for your money, either."

He hugged her sadly. "And I love you. I thought . . . oh, I don't know what I thought, but I've sure missed you, Tricia . . . and Bryan and Suzanne." Then Tricia heard him add softly, "And your mom . . ."

Tricia's heart filled with hope. "Maybe you could come back. Maybe go to counseling or something with Mom."

"Oh, Tricia," he whispered, almost like a sigh. But even in the dim light, he looked hopeful. "I see so much of Gramp's influence in you, especially that time you phoned me back here to ask my forgiveness."

Whew! she thought, grateful she'd listened to God's prompting that day. Smiling up at her father, she said, "It's really Jesus you are seeing in me, you know."

Dad nodded thoughtfully, then ruffled her hair and smiled—just like he used to do.

Tears burst into Tricia's eyes, and she hugged him again.

A while later, when he drove off, Tricia saw her friends waiting on their bikes by the orange trees, and Mr. and Mrs. LeRoy going into their house. *Lord, don't ever let me be such a disappointment to my grandparents,* she prayed as she went for her bike. *And help my dad learn to know you!*

In the darkness, it seemed as if God answered, *Trust in me . . . trust in me in all things.*

She grinned, then dragged her bike out from behind an orange tree. Climbing on, she called out to her friends, "Hurray for the Twelve Candles Club!"

"Hurray!" they all cheered.

"Let's ride!" Jess proclaimed, and they all laughed with her.

Tricia bicycled down the driveway with them, the wind blowing in her hair and joy rising in her heart. The poem came again, and she recited it as if it were a gift for her friends. . . .

"How do you like to go up in a swing, up in the air so blue? Oh, I do think it the pleasantest thing ever a child can do! Up in the air and over the walls, till I can see so wide . . . till I look down on the garden green, down on the roof so brown. Up in the air I go flying again, up in the air and down!"

———

Melanie Lin has just moved into Santa Rosita Estates and wants nothing more than to be a part of the Twelve Candles Club. But Melanie's worried that her Chinese heritage will keep her from fitting in.

When the TCCers learn Melanie is a model, they are very impressed. Melanie offers to get modeling jobs for her new friends, but when she sees with her own eyes their lack of modeling skills, it looks like Melanie's idea is a disaster. See what happens in book five of THE TWELVE CANDLES CLUB, *Melanie and the Modeling Mess.*